GOING TO THE MOON

The Hosanna Man
Common People
Native Ground
A Pledge for the Earth
The Honeymooners (play)
Turning Point
Clipped Wings
The Real Life
In My Own Land

PHILIP CALLOW

—

Going to the Moon

MACGIBBON & KEE

First published 1968 by MacGibbon & Kee Limited
1-3 Upper James Street Golden Square London W1
Copyright © Philip Callow 1968
Printed in Great Britain by
Bristol Typesetting Company Limited
Barton Manor - St. Philips
Bristol 2

SBN : 261.62077.0

BR/BR

We are going to the moon . . .
ANAIS NIN

GOING TO THE MOON

I

THAT's life : we must get going. Can't wait. Century on century, pressing out of the mothers. Sex is a necessary crime.

Before I left school my mother gave me a piece of paper with the 'facts of life' scribbled on, and told me to read it out in the lavatory and then flush it away, quick. Mystified, slightly sick in advance, I went into the backyard, shut myself in the reading room and read the scrap of paper. It said something like—' The man puts his thing into the woman's thing, and makes babies.' Immediately I felt dirty, contaminated by this horrible shithouse secret. I dropped the paper hastily, watched it flutter into the pan and float. I dragged on the chain in a panic, came out and didn't go back in the house. I burned with shame at the thought of facing my mother, burned with her shame as well as my own.

Not long after this the war started. I was nearly fifteen, in four months I'd be at work. With my brother, younger than me, I was evacuated to some indifferent relatives who had a caravan in the country. Being sensitive kids we knew we weren't wanted, which made our homesickness worse. Before on holidays it had been a marvellous spot, the river down below your feet, at the end of the day the fields and thistles and flickering rabbits all still, and you swam and floated in the strange evening peace, wanting to stand still, wanting to whisper. Now I hated it all, lying in the bunk in the mornings listening to Tommy Handley on the battery radio up on the shelf, waiting to be called, and told, while they made the breakfast. We howled to come home as soon as our mother visited us. Alan had put his legs into a sleeping bag and it was full of dead wasps. He was stung all over. So an uncle came, Geoff the factory worker, he worked in a car factory and he took us back in his car to the factory town we were suddenly passionate to see again, which was in a hollow anyway and the Germans wouldn't find it.

They found it and they found my father: nearly dropping a land mine on him. He was a warden, the ARP post
was at the corner of Ernaldlhay Street, in St Stephen's
School. I used to go and play table tennis with him in the
very classroom I'd known as a schoolboy. It was a weird
sensation, standing on the old uneven boards and trying
to visualise how it had been—and then trying to stop it
coming back, trying not to remember: this was all wrong,
a joke, it had to mean more than this, surely? I stared
round at the shrunken room, flaking cream distemper on the
walls, the map of the world spattered with red bits, the iron
stove that used to be the very core of the room, the heart
of my life, it glowed, it burned, it was alive, a mess of coke
dust around the base inside the wire cage—and look at it
now, dead as a drainpipe, shorn of beauty. An electric
fire plugged in by the side of it, where the scuttle of coke
used to be. I kept struggling in spite of myself to recreate
everything. The desks had all been cleared out, men in
rubber boots and greatcoats sat round drinking tea, playing
cards, smoking fags—nothing was left of my world. This
was like a dream, I walked in and out of it, played ping
pong against my Dad who was different, bluff and slightly
impersonal among the others, who danced about youthfully,
all arms and legs at the other end of the table shouting
'Wake up, dreamy! You've got a hole in yer bat, son!' I
was dreamy because it was a dream: one day I'd wake
up.

Then the land mine floated down, while I was in the
shelter with my mother, brother, and two or three people
from across the street. The floor moved, and the bunks, as
if we were riding a wave that bulged through the ground
and went on and on until there was no more earth. Someone started to whimper, then a tinkle of water in the dark.
One of the girls from over the street was pissing in our
enamel pot.

Afterwards my mother went looking for my father, found
the school smashed and asked a policeman. 'If he's dis-
eased'—meaning deceased—'he'll be at London Road'.
This was a joke we repeated grimly for a long time after,
when things were in one piece again. It was a kind of

8

shorthand, perfect for getting across to people at one stroke how horrible and daft and *the same* things were during the bombing. As a joke though it was lousy—you had to explain what was meant. Nobody got it the first time.

When we found the right hospital and got in to see my father, he'd been cleaned up. Still it scared me stiff, seeing him there with his head smothered in bandages, his face naked and helpless without glasses, his voice quavery as the thread of life. I wanted to sob, I wanted to leave. I stood and stared. The school wall had collapsed on him, buried him, filled his mouth with rubble and smashed his false teeth. The dirt blinded him. His jaw was splintered and fractured, nothing else. Only it was. The old life was smashed to bits that night, and for good. Fatherless, we shifted to Lillington and lived there throughout the war. After several months at a special hospital at Bromsgrove my father joined us again—we had some rooms in a basement—and the night of the blitz came. Next morning I was pedalling hard to work as usual and got turned back at a roadblock. The centre was a shambles, fires still blazed, the whole shopping district had been gutted, they were still digging out the bodies. Nothing of this affected me, except vaguely as an excitement. Funny thing this is: it was my home town and yet the raid had missed me and I couldn't feel it. The final, terrible thing had happened already, now I was broken away; I belonged somewhere else.

And that was what they were telling me at the roadblock. Go back—and I thought I heard the word corpses. I'd never seen a corpse in my life. I showed my identity card. 'You can't come through here this morning, nobody can,' the man said, important with it. I didn't need telling twice: wheeled round, the tyres sang hooray, long live the blitz, my legs pushed harder than ever, and willingly. Going in the opposite direction I opened my eyes and marvelled, and saw what a wonderful road it was. Freedom— the same road, only in the opposite direction. What beauty it had now, how it invited, opened, led on. The same road: I couldn't get over that.

Those war years, all that period in the basement, shuttling across the fields through the lands and old hamlets to the brand-new factory on Hammer Lane, opposite Ferguson's, acres of that, with Geoff in there somewhere—to and fro between factory and basement, then the daylight on Saturday, half day, falling asleep in broad daylight on the bus going home, tired out. Yet when I think of it now it was a sort of trance-like waiting time, snug really. The sirens wailing before six at night and the guns around the city letting off crumps sometimes before I'd even got over the bridge across the river and up Warmeleigh Hill alongside the park, pushing my bike and with my back to it all, never looking back. Too scared. But snug because I was on the way home, I knew where I belonged, I had no girls, no personal problems. Getting the taste for solitude early, my beam slicing the night in front of my wheel as the searchlights sliced at sky behind me, over the city : turning the bike into a companion, listening to noises of complaints, tell-tale rattles, liking it for carrying me, wanting to coax it like an animal.

Later on, when the raids got worse, you could see long queues at the bus station every night waiting for the Midland Red to take them out of it. There was talk of the anti-aircraft guns running out of shells, fighters clustered around London and Buckingham Palace and none left for the Midlands, none in the air over the provinces—there was a lot of dull bitterness and the queues were growing. They carried bundles of blankets like refugees, plenty of them : the story goes that they knocked on doors up and down Lillington and the sods wouldn't let them stay. I don't know, I was in a trance, I kept pedalling.

Towards the end of the war I was more restive, finding out things from books in queer accidents, with nobody to guide, advise or warn me. In the warm months I wandered in the fields and felt how lonely the summer was, and sat down by spinneys reading a soft warm weepy writer, Saroyan, for the first time, weeping inside like him and choking back love for every damn thing. It was a funny time. I got to know an apprentice in the factory, Barry Joy, an excitable, pop-eyed, superior lad, excited by the idea of young Ustinov in his white shirt, audacious as Orson Welles, and Barry talked very fast and rolled his eyes, watching for the foreman and keeping his machine working as he poured out this heady stuff about plays he was trying to write— plays!—and, very polite, would I have a glance at this article on Ustinov he'd ripped from a *Picture Post*. He kept harking back to his own efforts, modelled on those of his idol Ibsen, and to the symbolism of those great plays— ' great, Colin!'—with his tongue feverishly licking, the sly smile of conceit and ambition twitching up his lips. Then the foreman sails round the corner. ' Here the bastard comes—see you later.'

I was pure, in a trance. I never even masturbated. Once I was wandering up and down longingly outside a cinema and a G.I. took me in, paid for me and even bought me chocolate. Nothing else. All I said to him was ' Thank you ' and ' Cheerio '. That was to see Danny Kaye's first film *Up In Arms*. Another time I queued up in a Lillington side street to get into a fleapit where they were showing a for-bidden picture—I think Japanese. Remember nothing of it now, no details whatsoever, only the sensation of mystery, languor, filtered light, bamboo screens. Secrecy. More trance, drugging me. And now I was making the first feeble efforts to wake up, break out. I stood forlornly on a street corner one vacant Saturday afternoon, longing for something to happen to me.

Nearly every night I sat in the front bedroom of that basement working at a correspondence course for A.M.I.Mech.E. ' Success or No Fee ' and ' Let Me Be Your Father ' the advert had said. I slaved at it for a whole year, held my head and fought it, the solitary hero again, then abruptly threw in my hand and changed to a writers' school. I lasted four lessons, until my tutor told me I couldn't repeat myself in the same sentence, there was a rule. And other rules, about beginnings, middles and ends —rules for this and that. Good-bye, good-bye. Back with Saroyan in the grass, crying inside. Then in pure contrast to this I had a sudden burning passion for a motorbike. I belonged to a firewatching party, and I remember sitting up in a room at the top of the building where we lived, aching in every bone, nauseous, it was three in the morning and I was on duty: reading a textbook on the two-stroke motorbike, studying details of carburettor, plugs, the simple fundamentals. My father took me one Sunday to see a Velocette; fifteen pounds the man wanted. He wheeled it out of the shed, gave it a kick and the machine burst into life, deafening. I knew then I didn't like the reality at all, only the *idea* of a motorbike. The reality scared me. But it was too late now and anyway how could I explain it? Try it, have a run, the man was saying. I climbed on behind him, hugging the pillion with my legs to avoid having to clutch his mac too tightly; we went blasting through the streets in great style. I detested the fuss it made, the attention I felt sure we were getting. Then it was my father's turn for a trial run, squatting on the pillion rather than sitting because of his long legs. Off he went on the back, strangely wild-eyed, hair blowing, knees stuck out and the ends of his mac flapping. He came back excited, like a boy. I was the boy and I just stood there. What a fool. We hung about, hesitating, my father pretending to examine this and that, twitching at the sides of his trousers—I knew it took a long time for him to make a decision, these were the signs of him kneading one, forming words, but the man took it differently. 'Go on then, twelve quid—how about that?' We paid up and wheeled it away. The idea of having it, the practical side, fell through because when we enquired I was too young to be insured. So to make use of it as transport I rode pillion, my father taking me in each morning, dropping me off and then doubling back to reach his place. Long before it was time for me to take out a provisional licence and learn, I'd managed to drop hints about my lack of interest in motorbikes now. In the end somebody bought the Velocette for eight pounds.

I had a month off work with cardiac debility, exhausted by twenty-mile-a-day bike rides, and I lay in bed studying the stains and flaking plaster round the meter boxes, letting my mother dote on me. I read *Oliver Twist* in bed, I remember. Hot warm juicy tears rolled out, real ones. The doctor who examined me was a woman, Miss Laverty. She did her stuff with the stethoscope, then sent me out of the room while she talked to my mother. I liked her, she was human, not a bit like doctors I could remember as a child,

who stormed in like whirlwinds without knocking, barking
'Good morning' if you were lucky—and you were expected to leave the door off the catch for them. Hell, you
could no more think of them standing there on the doorstep banging than you could God Almighty. And, naturally, they were always late. The tension would be terrific;
it was like expecting royalty. My mother wasn't cowed or
overawed, even then, but she was clenched tight in readi-
ness—the strain showed on her face. It wasn't difficult
though to imagine the effect on some poor devils with less
independence. Christ knows what we had to be inde-
pendent about, we were poor enough. Yet we were, we all
had a touch of it, all thought something of ourselves—it
was in the family, a trait running right through. Those
were the days of the 'Panel' and the 'Box', words you
didn't need to understand or be told about, they were
dinned into you while you were in the pram near enough.
And clubs for this and that, Foresters, Hearts of Oak, Odd-
fellows, friendly societies, tiny insurances. Clubs were your
only real safeguard. My grandfather belonged to about six,
for sickness, death, old age, Christmas, holidays . . . there
was no end to it. But doctors . . . the first one I remember
was Dr Lamb. I didn't find him autocratic, I pitied him,
even at that age. His huge balding forehead used to wrinkle
convulsively all of a sudden, and the whole of his scalp
jerked helplessly, while his eyes screwed tight. It was shell-
shock, according to my mother. Of course, I was fascinated
to see it, this mixed in naturally at my age with the pity.
You used to wait for the next seizure, impatient for it to
happen. His great ugly hole of a waiting-room, that was a
place, gloomy as a free clinic. It echoed with feet and nervous coughs. When you tip-toed in you had to whisper up
and down the rows of hard chairs furtively, 'Who am I
next to, please?' My mother took me to Dr Lamb one day
for him to look at my cock, to see if it needed circumcising
or not. He pulled at it, let it lie in the palm of his hand,
dragged the skin back fastidiously, gave me a brief radiant
smile I've never forgotten and then he twitched, the foul
wince convulsed his face and buckled the skin of his skull
again. He still had hold of me. I felt terribly sorry for him.

I imagined his head bursting, ticking with too much brain.

'What d'you think, Doctor?' my mother was asking, red in the face with anxiety.

There was some discussion, more convulsions, but no, he didn't think it was necessary.

Out we came into the ugly street. Round the corner was a pill factory, stinking of chemicals, steam wafting out of the top windows. Courtaulds was another permanent stink, right across the other side of the town at Molesdale, towards the gasworks. If the wind was in your direction you caught the blended whiff of it, anywhere in the town.

When Dr Laverty called me back in, she strode up to me on her short thick legs and told me I had nothing to worry about (I wasn't worried because I was too young, and never stopped to think about funerals, death, heart failure applying to me), if I didn't do anything silly like running cross country races or swimming the Channel I'd live to a ripe old age. It was a matter of simple common sense. After all, she wouldn't dream of entering a beauty contest —'See what I mean?'—and with me on one side of her and my mother the other she put her arms round us, roughly, like a man. She was Irish, my mother said afterwards, as if that explained something.

2

IN paradise I was, if I'd only realised it, being at home and not sick, no pain, nothing the matter with me except that I was supposed to rest and eat butter and eggs and drink milk, build myself up. You must rest, my mother kept saying, and I sighed and muttered all right, as if it was something that went against the grain but I'd have a try. I was vaguely guilty, which added to the pleasure, and in a dim blurry way I knew I was in paradise, but I didn't seize it or say to myself how good if it only lasts. Very quickly I learned how to be slothful, how to take things easy. It was easy! Life was simple, no problems, not a worry in sight, and never, before or since, have I got on so well with my mother, never been so yielding, tender, so ready to agree, so eager to make her happy. Those lovely tranquil spells in the afternoons of a mellow September, still, smoky weather, leaves falling easily and rustling, keeping the peace, what did we do with ourselves except read, and wander out for walks down to the river, through the park, or go to the pictures and see something like *Mrs Miniver*. One afternoon I painted the shutters with cream paint in the living-room—indoor shutters they were, and it was cream she wanted, not white—while she sat reading her library book, and it would be a title so typical of her, so characteristic, say *One Pair of Hands* or *My Turn to Make the Tea*. Or we would go out shopping, me carrying the basket and walking on the outside in a proper manner. As we walked we passed comments, gossiped, made little jokes, and I saw how my mother glowed like the leaves, how vivid she was when she was happy, how alike we were in so many small ways. Truly we were in accord. All we needed was time, with the pressure blissfully off. It was good and it was beautiful while it lasted.

A year or so later I was off again, but only for a few days—the machine oil had given me a rash on the hands and arms. Instead of winning me some time, it got me transferred to another job, that's all. For some reason I can't remember we had changed doctors, perhaps because the new one was nearer to where we lived. So I sat in the tomb-like silence of this strange waiting-room one evening with dermatitis fingers itching, vile, bandaged—then up three stairs and in to his room when it came to my turn. A great difference, a revelation. A big expanse of thick carpet and then the huge desk across one dimmed corner, the table lamp softly shedding gold light, plummy velvet curtains to the left covering the french windows, brushing the floor. Nothing humane and jolly like Dr Laverty; this was different altogether. But very impressive. I had a feeling of grand proportions, authority, dignity, absolute calm and complete mastery over all our woes. And I'd brought my itchy fingers! The doctor was foreign, a sharp kindly man who preferred I think to maintain a professional distance between him and his patients. That was what the desk was there for. Strangely enough, I didn't resent it, and I liked him. I liked him very much. He had an instinctive grasp of character I felt, as his eyes watched me, as he examined me. I felt taken into account as a human being, and that's rare.

One day at the factory the sirens sang out in broad daylight, before dinner-time. Men straightened up from their machines, looking puzzled. Then the machines cut dead, over our heads the shafts stopped twirling, the belts slowed, flapped and hung quiet, there was the moment of portentous silence this killing of the power always created, and suddenly everybody was running like mad, crouching against the blast wall built against the stores pen. They must have heard a plane; I didn't. There was a crash, over in a far corner of the main shop, glass dropping, somebody shouting ' All right, don't panic, he's gone now—walk out to the shelters.' This was a good distance, out through the yards past the cycle racks, the cyanide and sandblasting sheds, through the gates where the works police lived in their concrete pillbox stinking of tobacco, sweat, bad breath, with the slits for windows, and across to a brick surface shelter in a bit of waste ground. We trooped out in the wintry light, staring round like convicts being taken for exercise, blinking up at the sky.

' There the bugger is !' a bloke yelled. We bent double and ran the last few yards, diving for the shelter doorway. I heard some ragged machine-gun fire, *tock-tock*, *tock-tock*, from the Home Guard on the top of Ferguson's roof—they'd let fly at a Whitley or a Wellington by mistake the week before, it was a great joke—out of the corner of my eye I saw it, lots of us did, circling slowly and banking, so casual; fascinated, I saw the black markings clearly as it made off. It seemed in no hurry. ' See the cheeky sod? See 'im?' everybody was saying, full of wonder and admiration.

3

SUBMERGED, it floats up, refracted. Faces, hundreds of faces, a buzzing hive of lives. Fragments, nothing permanent or ever likely to be, and you accepted it that way and lived it. What else was there? Nobody stopped to question, there was a ration even on questions. You kept dodging, living. War or no war, you hung on for the Saturdays and the holidays and the pension. Roll on the daylight.

Robust, ugly, close, describes the life around me as a kid and in youth, but my life in it fluttered like a candle, tremulous, delicate and supple in the draughts. The bomb blasts, incendiary raids, sirens shrieking, flames roaring—none of it toughened me. I seemed queerly immune. I stayed the same skinned rabbit. Funny thing was, the bombs didn't frighten me half as much as school did—the one I played truant from—where they got their hooks in you and made you tremble by looking at you in a certain way, even if they didn't do anything much. They had absolute power, that was what their look meant when they unmasked it, which they did, cruelly and cunningly and without any betraying words, for you and nobody else. And it followed you home, this dreaded blazing look of power, it waited for you at night, in dark corners of your bedroom, especially Sunday night lying in bed. You could feel them then, waiting, with that terrible power they had which you never hoped to explain, which nobody else suspected or would ever believe in. So you wept, hard and bitter into the pillow. You were lost. You knew there was no hope because that was what it meant, being lost. Perhaps by the time the Germans came, with that heavy pulsed engine sound we used to identify, lying under it in the Anderson, listening intently with our whole bodies—perhaps then I'd used up my terror. But I was born frightened. Pushing my bike out, climbing the cellar steps with it and getting on, feeling the balancing thinness of it under me in the dark, seven in the morning, earlier, pointing it at the city in the freezing fog I rode along in a quiver of fear and excitement. I was more alive than others because more afraid. Afraid of ice on the road, afraid of being late, afraid of shapes, noise, birds, cattle, vivid with fear and expectation. I chewed the rime of frost on the mouth-opening of my balaclava, made it warm and moist, listened for the knock in the bottom bearing as my pedals drove round, as the faulty dynamo hummed me along and the dark opened for me and swished shut again behind my saddlebag, friendly at the front and venomous in the rear, the hedges menacing and wet and fog-rotten, hanging over.

4

IT was really a cellar, a dugout, our home during the war: once the servants' quarters to the big house up above which was now split into flats. In the buttressed passage was a board on the wall with a row of bells for calling whoever they needed—now disused, rusty, covered in a film of dirty cobwebs. The relatives nearby who had found us the place, they were snug and snotty as ever in a well-upholstered flat. How it must have been rubbed in to my mother, arriving there with a van-load of trashy, worn-out possessions, two boys and no husband—no wonder she looked round once in that draughty, damp hole in the ground and burst into tears. Up above—that was the thing!—in the next street, the rich relatives and their thick carpets, ivory paint, revolving bookcases, standard lamps, and—the thing that made a big impression on me—a row of gay tins on a shelf in the kitchen, labelled ' Sugar ', ' Coffee ', ' Flour ' and so on. All so gay and orderly and undisturbed, war or no war. They were up there so they had to look down. To be poor had been meaningless to me until then. I moved from house to house, street to street in the early days and it was the same element I swam in. No shame, no strain. Kids accept whatever they find anyhow—and we'd been on visits to these prosperous relatives at Lillington now and then, even slept in the richery once or twice, and I played with my cousins, two girls, holding them down on the bed, pinning their arms and feeling a strange excitement because they were girls, they smelled different, laughed different, and their father came in at night when we were having tea, immaculate at cuffs and collar, his suit a subtle shade of brown. He made his entrance rubbing his hands and chuckling in a peculiar way, as if he was telling a dirty joke to himself. His top lip fascinated me, it looked so sore around his Ronald Colman moustache, it was bright red on a white puffy face. He was a store manager with a flair for window dressing. The reps called in droves, especially around Christmas time, showered him with gifts and plied him with drinks. That was no doubt why his lip looked sore, he had a habit of sucking it after it had soaked well in the whisky. His firm, a big one with branches everywhere, sent him in a firm's car to conferences in London and the south. He was a big man, with bull-frog eyes trained on you coldly. He could deliver an opinion on any subject and sound authoritative, he could fix a car, an electrical gadget, a radio, he was organised and tuned in. A mixer, a man of the world. At home we called him Chief, he was such a big-head.

My mother burst into tears that first night in the cellar. I got it then in a flash, the bitter caste system, the up there and down here and half-ways, and Christ knows how many graduations in between. My mother felt the weight of it, I could see: I was terribly depressed. Yet what a cosy place she made of that hole, and when my Dad came out of hospital he was soon painting doors, walls, boarding over the great iron range the servants had cooked on for the upstairs people, getting a slow combustion stove installed—*The Otto*—and it was all different; transformed. No more inferiority. He just wasn't aware of it himself, he was too unworldly. So a clean feeling came in with him. When the bombers were going over in droves to Coventry they didn't feel too happy upstairs either, the flat owners and poodle fanciers, and on one occasion when the shit was falling a bit close—probably jettisoned by a stray plane— they were soon down banging on the door at the bottom of the area steps. My mother rushed to let them in. I'd have been hard of hearing for a while if it was me.

Coombe Park. I liked it very much, it was just the people. The whole town was like that, it had a reputation in the Midlands. We soon saw that it was the top end where we lived that was like it, not down the bottom past the theatre, under the arch and on the other side of the railway bridge. That was where the gasometer and coal yard and factories and working people had been shoved, in a stink of gas and glue. It was in two distinct halves, this town, amazingly. Up at the top were wide streets planted with trees, chestnuts mostly. No rough kids, no parks: instead there were gardens and tennis courts, railed off, and a key for residents. I liked it though. It had a spacious feeling.

I began to buy a book now and then, getting them direct from publishers. Brand new—send me so-and-so. I wasn't doing anything with my money, no girls, drinks, records, and although it was a pittance, my apprentice pay, after I gave my mother some I still seemed to have plenty. Without knowing it hardly, in that same trance state, I was building up a little nucleus of a new world, different, dangerous, explosive, called a library. I bought Saroyan, Ethel Mannin, I bought Arturo Barea's trilogy—the lot in one go. That was exciting when the parcel came, the Faber label on the brown paper, and inside the cocoon, tightly pressed together, mint, the three books—*The Root*, *The Forge*, *The Track*. I think that was it. I can remember the smell of the new print better than the titles or the contents, the crisp paper, uncut pages ragged in the middle. It was wartime, the paper was terrible utility stuff, greyish lavatory paper. But it still looked good.

It could have been about this time that my parents started to worry about the way I was going, my isolation, solitary habits, avid reading and all that. Nothing was said, but one Saturday afternoon my father turned up with a friend, a workmate from his office, who brought his young daughter along, a girl of roughly my own age. She was shy, tall, a reader like me, and she wrote poems, apparently—wasn't that a coincidence! I could see she was a lonely bird and all she wanted was to stay that way; I think she realised too as soon as she set eyes on me that we were in the same boat. What did parents know about it? Blushing, she held out a collection of Chinese short stories she had brought along for me to borrow, that is if I'd like to borrow them. Sorry for her, I went to the bookshelf and got down the Ethel Mannin, *No More Mimosa*—could I lend her that? Yes, thank you ever so much. A murmur, scarcely moving her lips. So we sat there in frozen silence, such a farce, a fiasco, and waited to be left alone again, for them to all clear off and leave me alone, my father yapping happy and oblivious, my mother rattling cups and plates in the kitchen—my mother who loved her solitude as much as I did. She understood me through and through, I was certain of it, but she daren't approve, and it wasn't natural. But I knew damn well she was in there putting up with it, praying for the time to go, like I was. Another shy violet, another deep one.

At the factory I had mates among the apprentices, a few, but when I reached Lillington at nights and week-ends there was absolutely nobody. And it was the truth, mostly I liked it better on my own. The library, the Reference, a bookshop in the High Street, going to the pictures down by the river, or by the station, sitting in the dark wrapped in fantasies. Coming out was grisly, reality was always worse afterwards, drearier and more ugly because for that couple of hours you had really escaped, slipped the leash, as surely as if you'd been to an opium den. And like any other habit-forming drug it kept dragging you back in, magnetic. I felt remorse sometimes when I came out, grudging the waste of time, of life. It was beginning to grow in me, the necessity to do something, make something, use my life. Still I couldn't break the habit, it had started far too early, when I was eight or nine and the Prince of Wales was at the bottom of our street, Ernaldlhay Street, the gilt and plush fleapit where I went Saturday afternoons for the tuppenny rushes. Orange peel and silver paper flicking through the magic beam, deafening cheers in the serial, the Yankee cavalry thundering to the rescue in a majesty of pennants and uniforms and flashing hooves.

Later on it would be other palaces, the Globe, Scala, Gaumont, Palladium, Crown, Astoria, Regent—there must have been a couple of dozen nearly and I visited each one in turn, ringing the changes, even coming out half-way through a programme and changing to another cinema if I was very restless or just couldn't stick it. And kept this up every week, year in and year out, two or three times a week, tramping out to trim suburbs, slum districts, factory areas, waste lands, winter and summer—a real addict. (One of the first stories I ever wrote was on the subject of this pernicious habit—called 'Twice a Week or Three Times'.) An avalanche of films, comedy, drama, news—most of it trash, utterly forgotten now. The influence on me and kids like me at this tender, impressionable age must be incalculable. I had constantly changing heroes and heroines, and some steadfast ones, like Henry Fonda, who still cast a spell now, though not strongly enough to drag me inside. Some films, like *The Al Jolson Story*, I'd see again and again. If it had an idol in it then I'd go anywhere, whatever it was—the very thought of a Fonda, a Gary Cooper, their aura, would be enough to force me out there, sometimes dragging my feet. It was worship, I was worshipping, adoring; these tatty temples where I attended to my devotions and begrudged the time bitterly afterwards, they enslaved me more than factories and offices ever did, and I poured some of the best of myself out there, in the cosy dark smelling of Flit. All my ardent desires, rebellion, rejection, all the fervour of youth, need for Something, idealism, the longing to enshrine and dedicate, all the marvellous love I was aching to give somebody.

5

OFTEN I'd be lonelier with pals than on my own. It was being forced home slowly, slow and steady, and I knew it but wasn't ready to admit it yet, that I couldn't hit it off with anybody; though most people I found seemed to like me. But I would find out soon enough, it had to be special pals, and there weren't many.

I was in the middle of the war, had seen the red glow in the sky from Lillington, firewatching at the top of the building, heard the dull thunder of guns, bombs, mines and heard them say 'They've had it.' It was blitzed, obliterated, but I was still going there every weekday, working, and I came in along the big new highway that went cutting across the main road towards Alvington, bypassing the city; so there was no reason for me to go into the city centre. I never did, until after the war. The city was blitzed; that meant the centre mainly, all the shops gone. People were still living there in their thousands, the factory filled up with them just the same. What did they mean, blitzed? I seemed devoid of curiosity: no interest in the smoking ruins, rubble and slag of shops, the gutted Council House. I kept coming in along the raw swooping bypass that was like a landing strip, rudimentary; past the barrage balloon and the Pioneer Corps, the derelict farm next to the cardboard box factory, the Highwayman, up and down on the last lap with aching legs, over that sod of a hill over the canal, the hump of the bridge, then the spread of factories before me and I could lean back sighing luxuriously and freewheel, sailing to the bottom; then sharp left at the chip shop for the gates, the bike sheds.

Dinner-times I mooched around the side streets with a little knot of apprentices, killing time and digesting the canteen dinner, or we stayed on in the canteen pulling faces at the screeches of some luckless soprano in the ENSA concert, grinning and feeling embarrassed when the blokes lost patience and banged their plates on the table, yelling insults, or just turned their backs and played cards, refusing to clap the acts. The regimental bands were something else, they had a fierce blaze of noise and power and that dominated, compelled attention. They were smart, disciplined, uniformed, they went into action like machine parts, the bandmaster jerking them along inhumanly, working the controls. It was beautifully co-ordinated, a precision job, and it was fiery and martial, conquering the din and forcing respect. Everybody liked the excitement and glamour and the fact that it was depersonalised; nobody making any personal appeals, nobody making themselves look cheap and daft, soliciting for claps. This was professional so you didn't have to worry.

I went on holiday with four apprentices, just as if it was peacetime. Somebody had the idea of hiring a boat, a yacht, where you could live on board, sleep and cook your food without any interference from adults. It sounded great. So that summer we went off to Leicester, changed buses for Nottingham, then out to Radcliffe in a taxi, in grand style. I was the only one with any experience of sailing—one or two holidays on the Broads as a boy with

Geoff, my uncle—but the others were falling over themselves to have a bash, drag on the ropes, hold the tiller, shout Help; anything. In a few hours on the wide brown river, amazing, we'd got the hang of it roughly; enough to set sail immediately for Nottingham, winding about through the flat meadows, semi-industrial and derelict-looking as we drew nearer, navigating two locks and nearly crashing the top of the mast against an iron bridge we thought looked high enough to float under. I was at the tiller, asking Johnny and Bob if we were clear as we slid closer; ten yards, nine, eight, seven—then they saw it wouldn't clear, no go, we were at least a foot too tall. No brakes. Stop—turn it round! they were squealing, running for the long pole, while I pushed desperately on the tiller and watched us spin, inches from the bridge.

Before we reached Nottingham Johnny had managed to cut his arm on the glass globe of the butane lamp in the cabin—he was trying to change the charred mantle.

'How in Christ's name did you do it?' Bob kept asking.

'I keep telling you—the glass was cracking—a big crack down the side of the bastard thing! It came to bits in my hand, I tell you!'

'How did you cut your bleeding stupid arm, then?'

'Oh Christ, listen to him. I done it, that's all I know—I done it!'

He looked so white-faced as we moored up at the concrete steps that we were scared: somebody ran off in a panic and called an ambulance while Johnny sat on the pavement outside a tobacconist's, feeling groggy. The woman inside brought out a little hard chair and got him on that. Soon the ambulance rushed up and we were all sitting in it, clanging through the streets of this unknown city. At the hospital Johnny was fine again, laughing round, but they made him go in and have the gash washed and dressed. Then we sauntered back all free and curious through the streets in the vague direction of the river, plenty of time, staring round and gaping at things. Our legs felt queer, from being several hours afloat. By the time we found the boat the feeling had worn off. I was sorry. I had felt unique like that, and it sent us into fits of laughter, the way we rolled and swayed like drunks. We did get drunk at a riverside village later, me for the first time. I drank five or six half-pints and lost control of my legs; I could think and see all right. We wandered back to the boat, testing each other on white lines, balancing on the edges of kerbs, and I seemed to be wading fatuously in the air, which was a thick substance. Lying in our bunks we kept roaring with laughter for no reason. I was happy, I felt at one with everybody.

Moored to the steps that first night at Bridgeford, near to where they played the tests, we decided to stay at Nottingham another night because the lads wanted to go to a dance at the Palais. I sat watching them getting ready; shoes being blacked and polished, Brylcreem rubbed in, combs flashing, clean shirts whipping out of the rucksacks like magic. Lou pranced around, enveloped in a snowy shirt that looked sizes too big for him until he folded back the cuffs, fastened them nattily with his chrome and mother-of-pearl links, slipped on his watch with the expanding chrome strap—all this before the crisp tails of his shirt disappeared into his pants. Tucking in his shirt he dug his hands down boisterously, right to the elbows, reaching under his crotch and grabbing the back flap. Then he buttoned up his flies and at the same time did a capering dance. Feeling the fresh shirt on his shoulders he crowed like a cock.

' Right, now then me cockers!'

He crouched like a boxer, leaned, punched the air, ducked, feinted. ' Where's the women!'

His black hair was flat on his head, slick with grease. It fitted him like a cap.

' Come on, come on,' Lou urged, on his toes now, punching.

' Ah belt up,' Johnny said from the mirror. He was studying a blackhead on his jaw and a fat pimple between his eyebrows that was festering. He touched the juicy yellow head of the pimple tenderly. ' You bastard,' he said softly, with respect.

' Who's ready then?' Eddie said, waiting to go, knocking

the dandruff off his shoulders for something to do. He had the middle button of his sports coat fastened and he looked a real dandy, his face sore and pink.

I wasn't going, I couldn't dance. The real reason was a crippling shyness and the fact that I was a late developer. Girls were a problem, another element entirely. I had no language I could talk to them in, it would be torment trying, so I kept right away. Instead I went to the pictures, to the Mechanics opposite Victoria Station. We'd arranged a taxi from there at eleven. When I came out there was still half an hour to wait before the lads turned up. It was dark, drizzling. To pass the time I headed up Mansfield Road in the warm rain, walking emptily in the strange dark into nowhere. I was nowhere, nothing. Clouds of a luxuriant loneliness drifting through me. Went past shops, alleys. Chemist on a corner. Church. Big hoarding at a junction. Avenue of trees and grass and a path up the middle, cutting through to the left, rising up a slope and going on, this swathe of green disappearing into the distance. Fantastic—seen nothing like it in the centre of a city. Went past, suddenly it was eerie. I was nowhere, nothing. I didn't belong here, I had nothing to do with these buildings, no connection with any of it. I stopped at another junction, peering this way and that. Where now? Straight on, that was safest. Felt lost already. So this was Nottingham. I would meet people here, vital things would happen, but I wasn't to know that. Peering up Mansfield Road I couldn't see anything; the street lights made a hole and the street went on and on, enormous, tunnelling northwards into nothing. I swung back and walked quickly downhill again to the pick-up place. Traffic, people had an air of menace, it was like being stranded on another planet. I saw the clock lit up on the station tower, still a long way off. Bleak, I made for that.

They turned up with a girl; she was having a lift in the taxi as far as the Bridges. Flushed with triumph, they were. I was glad to see them. We piled in the back, jammed tight, the driver saying something in his broad Nottingham. We bashed through the town, skirting the empty square; shooting down the narrow streets made the speed seem hectic. I was lost again. The girl was giggling, pressed up against me, hip bones grinding together. 'Hello, handsome,' she cooed, and she put her hand to my chin and stroked it, to feel the bristles. I hadn't started to shave, I was eighteen. 'Rough,' the girl said softly. I was struck dumb. No girl had ever touched me before. I smiled like a loony, smiled and smiled, blissful and foolish, smiling. I was in a tumult.

6

THE summer holidays. Still innocent, but the days of real innocence are over now, the camps by the river with the family, my mother and father, brother, sometimes the old man as well. My mother's father, a short, dark, deaf, smouldery man, a cinder of a man: a labourer, a diabetic. The Old Sweat, they called him; it didn't matter, he was deaf. He worked at any kind of labouring job, over acid vats in a plating shop, as a dustman, an ice-cream seller, Stop Me and Buy One. Ringing his bell, he swung round the corner, slow and steady, his short legs going at it, pushing his burden fixed in front, that heavy white box. Pushing and pushing for dear life, uphill and against head winds, when he would be forced to dismount and nearly crouch, get his shoulder to it. Pushing, pushing, as if he was building the Pyramids. On commission. He stopped at the end of our entry, we'd rush out and grab his offerings, frozen fruits. On he went slower than ever in his funny get-up, peaked cap and white coat, struggling to get it moving, overcome the inertia. He hitched about on the saddle like a boy to keep his feet on the pedals.

Sometimes he came with us on holidays. Usually though, at camps, it was just the four of us. Orford, and Stratford, and once to the Isle of Man. Orford was the one shining idyllic place. The whole area is effulgent now like a Blake engraving, the village, the road, the bridge, the ford, the baker's shop, the meadows and oaks and chestnuts, willows, the river with its weeds, currents, shallows, pebbles, rapids, rushes, mud, minnows. Even the haulage depot just outside the village on the way to the ford, where the heavy lorries were parked, and cattle trucks. And the farmyard and dairy, the lovely country stink, carts and animals and gateposts sunk in stillness those hot drowsing summer afternoons, when a creaking peace descended and you walked scuffing your feet, in old canvas plimsolls, feeling wholesome and in paradise as only a town boy can. Orford was the one absolute paradise place. Others had fragments, there it was complete, a world. Once we stopped going there it was lost, it never came again. Stratford we had to share with hundreds, it was a bit like the banks of the Ganges. Half the Black Country seemed to pack in there. Still it was fine, lovely. The idyll even came back in snatches there, early in the morning with the mist lifting on the brown water, when you smelled the bacon and heard it sizzle, heard them pump at the primuses. ' This is the life !' my father would say, wolfing his breakfast in the open air, his eyes gleaming, head turning as he scanned the multitude. An army of peaceful townies, more than half Brummies, under canvas : all shapes and sizes of tents, some elaborate constructions with flysheets and porches—with just enough space between each to stretch the guy ropes. They were all stirring, up making breakfast, on the way to fetch water, milk, to the camp store, some arriving in old limping cars loaded with equipment, springs groaning as they edged round in search of a space. It was a temporary township, and it had an itinerant, circus atmosphere I liked. It was organised in a loose, free-and-easy way, there was a camp shop, brick lavatories, you could hire a float and paddle up the river as far as you wanted, dragging it through the shallows. It was good, but not the same. Orford was real country, empty flat fields and nobody there but us. Paradisal. You were aware of insects, birds, particles of dust, fissures in the ground. A goat, that came up and ate anything, wisp of beard and crafty yellow eyes like a farmer. We made a mascot of him, half frightened at first, sat on his back and clung to his curved horns. He stood there, submissive as a donkey. Only at twilight he went mad when the devil seemed to get into him. He caught my father fishing down at the river bank, and once he lowered his head like a bull and came belting after my mother as she crossed the farmyard coming back from the shops. She yelled for help and ran for it—I forget how it ended. The farmer was friendly, always stopping to pass the time of day, and his ' Windy betimes ' joined the stock phrases of our household. Back home we repeated it as a joke, but it was more than that. Talismanic. Whenever we said it, in our attempt at a country accent, we were back there. For a short time. The life of the street blunted it soon enough. The welter of days and the racket drowned it. School hammered it into the ground.

7

OTHER holidays are obscure, the details foggy, the journey mysterious. It was nearly always camping, the only holiday we could afford in those days, but once it was to a Co-op camp outside Rhyl, in a big wooden hut that got roasting hot, in a flat dusty field, flat as a billiard table at the edge of the sand. The place was a sort of primitive Butlin's—no amusements. If there was any organisation I was too young to remember. The heat I remember—everything got burning hot. Sand, field, hut. The camp was a cluster of chalets in a wide square, open at one side. You went out through the opening in the grass bank and carried back your water from the standpipe by the fence, sometimes queuing for it. Queuing happily, smiling and chatting and letting another take your turn if they were in a hurry, because it didn't matter, you were benign and your whole personality changed when you were on holiday.

My father's back was burnt badly before we had been there a couple of days; my mother oiled it, dabbing the blistered skin, but it was too late, I heard him tossing and groaning in the middle of the night. Before that happened, he waded into the sea with my brother on his back. The sea glistened, almost oily with heat, swelled and pulled gently, creamed and frothed around your toes. It was white sand, a tropical holiday. My brother screamed, being carried into the water, screamed so loud it reached my mother sitting far back on the beach, but my father plodded on just the same, until my mother screamed as well.

' Don't be a fool,' she kept saying to him afterwards. ' He's only four, couldn't you *see* he was frightened?'

' How could I,' shouting, ' he was on me back!'

' Hear then—couldn't you hear him? Were you deaf or what?'

' And daft,' he said bitterly.

' Well then, don't be so stupid.'

' It wasn't hurting him,' Dad muttered. ' I had him, he wasn't even wet.'

' Don't do it again, don't do it!' my mother yelled, red with heat, exasperation, worries.

She was a prime worrier, like her own mother, who died in her fifties, cancer of the throat, before I could have any memories of her. There was a story about her I kept hearing, of when she was at Rhyl herself once for a holiday with her husband—with the family. Getting off the coach and making wearily for the boarding house, she saw a banknote on the ground and picked it up : a fiver. A terrible, terrifying discovery, because it haunted her, she carried it around in her purse for several days, afraid of her very shadow. They were poor. Five pounds in those days was a small fortune, must have been. Should she give it up? Should they keep it? God knows, they could do with it. The misery of this crisis of conscience, this conflict between need and what was right and proper, it ruined their holiday, even after she'd gone to the police station and handed it over. She was a decent woman, she went to All Souls Church, she'd worried endlessly all her life. Imagine the predicament. My mother often repeated this pitiful tale, trotting it out grimly with obvious fondness. It illustrated for her with simple force the terrible fact of Money, the need for it, the lack of it, how it could dominate and destroy. And there was no need for an example, she was a living one herself. A beautiful text-book illustration. Apt. Look no further. Not my father, her. My father had the far-off looks, he dreamed up one scheme after another in his early manhood, while the spirit was still strong and defiant in him. His whole character veered towards independence, something a little different. He wanted to take the initiative, invent, start a business. But he had no ruthlessness or egocentricity, he was astonishingly naïve about the world, and trusting, when it came to people. He had no insight into character whatsoever. And there was my mother, acutely aware of dangers, of snares and snags and pitfalls, rats and twisters, a worrier, a dogged fighter when it came to a roof over our heads and food in our mouths; otherwise she went in fear and trembling of any straying from the known path. My mother with her bitterly apt and crushing examples. So the dreamer stayed buried in my father. It gave him a boyishness, a childlike quality.

There was also another side to him, or, now I know myself better I'm inclined to think it another symptom of his thwarted, baffled state: a growing irritability. As a father he could be stern, severe, but for a long time I had sensed the cause of it and took no notice. He was wiry, thin, with a caved-in chest, ribs showing, deep salt-cellars, but big-boned. Tall, well over six feet—when he came out of the Tanks after the war he nearly joined the Special Police with his army pal Jim Brennan—nearly went to Ireland with the Black and Tans. It's just as well he didn't, he'd soon have been in trouble there—his instincts kept him out of it. But irritable—bursts of wild, violent irritability as long as I can remember. Later, in my teens, I kicked and rebelled and he came to control it. But it was always there. Sitting at the table having a meal, one hand dangling in your lap, suddenly he'd lash out savagely with his foot under the table. ' Both hands!' he'd yell, eyes popping. The shock of it used to unnerve me, then I'd sit there hating him, nearly shaking with hate. I'd vow this and that, store it up with venom, one more injustice to be brought to account, but it was soon forgotten. How could I keep it going, when he had clearly forgotten it in a matter of seconds? It was how he'd been treated as a kid himself, most likely. This wasn't punishment or cold discipline, it was a hot flash of unpredictable rage. If he did dish out punishment he had to be goaded—I might be talking upstairs in bed with my brother, or having mad fits of giggles.

31

'Go to sleep—this is the last time! Hear me?' he'd roar. 'Yes,' we chorused, heard the stairs door crash for the fifth, sixth time; and although we knew the dangers it was irresistibly hilarious, singing out in harmony like that and then the door, the howl of rage, the crash. Five minutes later we were at it again, couldn't stop. All at once a thunderbolt up the stairs, the bedroom door flung open and Dad towering there, a slipper in one hand. He burst in on us in dead silence, pure retribution, too awful to gaze upon. Paralysed, we writhed in terror under his great bony hand as the arm with the slipper rose and fell, merciless. 'John, that's enough, stop it, oh God,' my mother screamed up the stairs. She had lost control at last, it was a force of vengeance now up there, so she played her last desperate card —hysterics. Much later, as we sobbed and recovered, each one hearing the other bitterly crying, the noise of it changing gradually to a gulping, convulsive sob that had lost its meaning—it had gone on so long it was an end in itself— my mother would creep up the stairs with a bit of supper and a glass of milk. More ghastly even than these disasters was one time when she tried to stop him getting up the stairs to us. Barring his way, that was an awful mistake. I heard them struggling, banging against the boards, my mother sobbing 'Don't' and 'You're hurting me' and his ugly, unrecognisable voice yelling 'Gerrout—gerrout'. My mother won though, I could hear her crying brokenly 'Oh God' and it was worse than if she'd let him come up and give us the slipper. I never once saw them come to blows, but in that scuffle at the bottom of the stairs he dragged her by the hair apparently in his struggle to get at us. Did my mother tell me that detail herself? I can't remember. How else would I know a thing like that?

As the oldest in his brood—three brothers and a sister— he had that firm, decisive, responsible air about him whenever they were gathered together, say at Christmas reunions, or if one of them called at the house, or was with us on some trip or other. Uncle Mike, Uncle Geoff, Auntie Caroline, John (Jack as he was called at work, and by his pal Jim Brennan)—all dreamy types in a way, but all very different. Of the three brothers I liked Geoff the best—

though this isn't fair, I can't separate my old man from his strict-father, slipper-wielding, ankle-kicking moods, and he could be so different, holding us at arm's length with his long arm, huge hand splayed out on our chest while we swung impotently at him in mock fights. Taking us fishing. Bike rides. But he was so distant most of the time, abstracted, silent behind the paper, or dropping off to sleep, tired out. A presence only. And this tendency increased, he grew shadowy with age.

Uncle Mike I admired—not that we saw a lot of him. Bright and breezy, sharp humorous eyes, buck teeth which increased his attractiveness for me—his mouth always seemed to be splitting in a grin. Shock of curly black hair brushed straight back. He'd bang on the front door with such a characteristic jaunty knock you'd know without opening it who it was—' It's our Mike '—and my mother would bustle through the house wiping her hands on her apron, muttering ' What does he want?' or ' Why doesn't he go round the back like everybody else?' or something equally complimentary. She muttered and moaned about him, his very name spelled selfishness to her, his knock meant ' I'm after something ', so she resented him on sight. But for all that she was no match for him face to face; he was too breezy, confident, too sure of his charms. ' Hallo Nell!' he'd twinkle, grinning shrewdly yet frankly—it was his frank egotism that got you—and before long she'd be offering a cup of tea. ' If there is one Nell ' he'd say, and the flash of charm, the wink, but not really listening, talking to John about something, the object of his visit—some tool he wanted to borrow. Of course my mother was right again, he never made social calls, his visits had an object, he was on the scrounge. She would rush in and out—' I'm busy, you'll have to excuse me '—hot in the face with trying to register her resentment. I didn't care, I liked him. ' How's life?' he'd ask me, or Alan, dragging off those massive gauntlets like funnels, leaving his cycle clips on because he wasn't staying, and if it was winter his thin vigorous body would be bundled in a thick tweed overcoat with a belt, the collar a bit yellowish. He had a green van, a three-wheeler without doors, and instead of a steering wheel the

c

33

handlebars and controls of a motorbike. In this he delivered his fruit and vegetables—he was in business out at Ashmoor in a harum-scarum sort of fashion—and once I went the rounds with him. Not helping, I must have been too young; just sitting there. The way he leapt out like a spring at each call and went bounding up to the house, round to the back of the van dragging boxes about, thumping back into the cockpit and spluttering off down the road again— I remember the hectic quality, nothing much else. And the antiquated motor horn, the way he squeezed at that black rubber bulb with great aplomb, grabbing at it and squeezing for all he was worth, as if he had hold of his wife's breast; mouthing a curse, his front teeth sticking out. His drive, impatience. And a touch of ruthlessness.

Going to his house one evening, on my first visit—I was on an errand—my Aunt Olive let me in, and in the living-room there was my Uncle Mike stretched out full length on the sofa, hands behind his head, wide awake. Apparently he did that, every night. I was astonished and very impressed. There was something oriental about it. To be able to relax completely in your own house like that was wonder and mystery enough, without anything else. One thing I knew for certain, it would never have been possible in our household. Never. My mother was such an ill-sitting hen, the very atmosphere she generated was against it. What's the matter, don't you feel well? she'd have wanted to know. No good pretending you were under the weather either. Go to bed then, that's the place. You're taking up too much room—I don't care if nobody else is in or not— somebody might want to come in and sit down. I want to clean round there—your legs are in the way! A shower of reasons, answers. To have somebody sprawled in the living-room, *her* living-room, would have been no good at all, simply unthinkable. Whoever it was, she'd have soon tidied them up. Relaxation in our house meant my father slipping off to sleep in front of the fire, stupefied by heat and fatigue, his paper crumpled, his head sagging, and it meant the Old Sweat on the other side of the fire, in his own armchair—remnant of his own household, on his own squashed, stinking cushion, encased in deafness, glasses

34

mended with cotton, reading his library books, his Edgar Wallace. My mother in the kitchen, naturally, working at the washing-up or ironing or making supper—any damn thing. The gospel of work, the guilt of idleness. Relaxation, what's that? Never, not in my vocabulary. I have to keep working, what would happen if I didn't? Who'd do all the work? Would your father do it? The Old Sweat, would he do it? What about the dinner, the dirt, the fire, the mess, the holes? What about your torn vests, your frayed collars, your pyjamas that need patching? How can I stop? Tell me, go on. You talk daft, daft. What about the beds, the crocks, the slops, the cobwebs? The song, flinty and self-righteous and unanswerable, hangs over the sink and never gets washed away. I bite my lip, sink my head lower over my homework, in the workhouse.

It all changes when Uncle Geoff wanders in, on his way to Ferguson's—he's on nights. Half awake, dopey, he brings a new atmosphere. If I'm out of the room, out of the house, I see his uncared-for bedstead of a bike first of all, propped against the bricks in the entry—and my spirit lifts. Coming in I can smell the aroma of the machine oil his arms and hands are soaked with, even before I'm through the door.

The very opposite of a work fiend, he sits in the first chair he comes to, against the door, and waits slothfully for a cup of tea.

' Where's Jack?'

' At work, where d'you think he is?'

' Oh ah.'

This is mechanical, his exchanges give no idea of his intelligence. He is no fool, but sluggish. He drifts, and lets everything drift. Perhaps spoiled—the only son who stays at home, hangs on, the last one, and gets waited on, his mother fetching and carrying for him as if he's still a boy, when he's in his thirties. His mother dies, his father, in the end he is reluctantly on his own. Still people look after him, somebody turns up. His whole life runs on like that, least line of resistance. He is shy, in a shell, and there he stays, peering out sleepily, more and more fixed in his bachelor habits. Something about him warns you off, says

Don't touch me. So you don't. That's all. It's just a pecu-
liarity, something you accept, that makes him what he is.
Nobody knows what he really feels, what goes on inside
him. He never lets on. Nobody dreams of asking. In a sense
a mystery man, yet transparent, helpless; not so much furtive as veiled. His eyes are like that, sleepy, hooded, and a
surprising flick to them now and then. Never a straight
gaze—always flick, flick, and away; timorous, veiled. Whatever secrets he has are locked away for life, unless a woman
unlocks them one day. Which seems doubtful. He sits in
our house for an hour or so nearly every day, on his way
to Ferguson's—or comes in Saturday nights occasionally
for a fish and chip supper. Pickles? Yes please. Vinegar?
Yes please. Doesn't lift a finger, waits, yet the curious
thing is it doesn't bother my mother, though sometimes she
puts on an irritated act with him. She's fond of him basically. He's been coming so long he's almost part of the
furniture. Passive, he puts up no resistance, gives in to her
and to everybody. But all the while he is going his own
way in his own style, own time, with the least possible
effort. He sits there sweetly spooning his tea in a queer
spinsterish fashion, as if guarding his cup; still young-look-
ing, scratching his short hair and leaning forward drowsily
to read a newspaper hung over a chair against the table,
just out of reach. Pasty-faced, Stan Laurel-ish.

' You're the limit, you are—here,' and she snatches at
the paper and half throws it at him.

' Ta,' and he's gone, utterly absorbed, lips puckered
absently at the hot tea, sucking it in gingerly.

What a contrast to this brother is my father, who does
everything thoroughly and looks after his things, takes care
of them—if it's a pair of shoes, for instance, he talks of the
need to ' feed the leather '. His bike is oiled and clean, so
are his tools. When the bike isn't in use for a long period
he slings it up carefully in the shed, on two hooks, to keep
the weight off the tyres. The army training keeps coming
out, and when the two of them are together in some activity
my dad turns into a ratty, overbearing sod from sheer irri-
tation, taking charge because he is the one with method
and a sense of purpose. ' How long's our Geoff going to be

—what the devil's he playing at?' And Geoff arrives, slothfully late as usual, rubbing the sleep out of his eyes, the
camping gear or whatever it is gets lashed on securely, and
my father is in charge.

'The boss is doing it,' says Geoff to my mother, out of
hearing. Then in strides my father, waving his exasperated
hands at us. Uncouth, officious, in this mood everybody dislikes him. He mouths: 'Come on if you're comin'!' and
my mother strikes back—'Who d'you think you're talking
to?' We climb in, the journey begins, Geoff drives, Dad
sullen and stiff-necked at the delay. From the very start the
trip is tainted.

8

JIM BRENNAN and his brothers had set themselves up in
business—car sales and contract repair work, a few de-
liveries—and finally my father joined them as manager at
their garage in Teddington Court, a little cobbled back
alley off the Birmingham Road at the top of Malpas Hill.
I used to take up his sandwiches now and then during the
school holidays. He'd be peering into the innards of a car,
engrossed, strictly in an amateur capacity: he looked after
the books, the queries, drivers' problems, wages, orders,
in a wood and glass pen tucked inside the garage itself but
lifted up on stilts, part of the petrol and oil smell. The
booth where he worked was a mess, spilling with paper,
overripe files, spikes loaded with invoices, bulldog clips
hanging on nails hammered into the framework. Jim Brennan, managing director, would come in and lounge in the
doorway, smoking; a big-faced, square-jawed, heavy man
with no fat, sure of himself. His nerves, if he had any, were
certainly not on the surface, like my father's—though it's
strange, I thought of Dad at the time as a strong man, not
nervy at all. At home he gave an impression of strength because he had a touch of the Victorian parent—'Your
father is asleep!'—but as soon as I contrast him with others
I see how nervy and twitchy he was. Jim Brennan didn't
have a grain of that kind of nerve: on the surface he

seemed barely alive, just breathing. His pale eyes glanced over the storm of papers in a bored way, and he was soon on the way out to his real interest, cars, engine parts. He'd nod at me and at my father and say ' Okay, Jack '. Sometimes they'd be in conference outside, in the alley of back-to-backs. My father would be talking away rapidly, concerned, agitated, and Jim Brennan nodding vaguely as if the problem was featherlight on his husky sloping shoulders, saying ' Okay, Jack, okay, we'll do that, yeh.' They had been close pals in the army; there was a sepia photo at home showing them both in uniform, soft caps, my father in steel-rimmed glasses, sitting down, and Jim Brennan standing beside him with his hand on his shoulder, a beefy hand to match those hulking shoulders, that great jaw like a boxer's. Now he had prospered and had a big new house behind Stanley Park that we were invited to visit ' any time '. ' Don't wait to be asked, come round any time, Jack.' My father, though, wanted to give us all a treat : he was as proud of this fairy palace as Jim was, and too naïve to see how the splendours of a detached, beautifully kept residence with central heating and God knows what else would upset my mother, how the space and furnishings would crucify her with embarrassment. He kept at her, determined to have his way for once, and she would fend him off with reasons, fears, excuses. ' He's only being polite,' she'd tell him. ' He doesn't really want us to come —it's just you that wants to go, poking your nose in . . . Well I don't, thank you.' Later on, weakening, she wailed plaintively, ' What can I wear?'

' Don't be so daft,' my father laughed, ' it's not royalty, it's Jim Brennan!'

' And his wife,' said my mother grimly.

One Saturday evening we went, me and my brother dressed to kill, my father leading the way up to the oak door, which was lit, as if he'd been there hundreds of times and this was merely one more visit. ' Don't stare,' my mother hissed at us in a final warning as we entered the blaze of electricity inside, ' it's rude!' We were there for an evening meal and to inspect and sample the wonders of the central heating, my father going down to see the boiler in the basement, as well as other marvels we had heard rumoured, such as parquet floors, fitted carpets, bathrooms. And apart from all this, the sudden transformation of a detached house, the kind of thing I'd only seen before from the outside, into a warm, spacious, elegant interior where people sat and ate and went to bed, people we actually knew—that was almost too much for me. So was the terrific dazing strain of that visit, the relief when we were outside again, trooping meekly down the gravel like visitors at the zoo, my father shouting out too loudly altogether in that superior residential district, ' Good-bye, good-bye—so long, Jim!' And the roughneck himself on the threshold with his wife, smiling, subtly transformed by his wealth and power out of all recognition.

It was while he was manager at Teddington Court—exalted title, poor pay—that we went to the Isle of Man one summer holiday, for a camping fortnight. The stuff had gone in advance in a tea chest, carefully packed and lashed and addressed, to the unknown site. We followed a week later, jammed in a small car from the garage, being delivered to Liverpool by Joe Brennan, one of the brothers. Joe driving. A cordial, phlegmatic man, beefy like all his tribe, wedged behind the wheel like a fixture and driving steady as a rock through the black night, up north through the Potteries, no mistakes, no faltering anywhere. He said with a laugh to my grandmother, when she asked him how on earth he didn't get lost with all the twists and turns in the dark, ' I could do it in me sleep just about—been up and down this road so many times.' They stopped once for me to clamber out stiff-legged and be sick on the grass verge, then it was dawn and strange country spreading out, mill chimneys, the bleak raw muck of the north, charred slums, miles of black terraces, a furnace pounding and belching flame, drop hammers smashing. We pulled up outside a door in the middle of all this, Joe's mother lived here, she'd have breakfast on the go for us, knowing we were coming. In we piled, and a little woman made a fuss of us at that hour, worn and haggard, in the eternal pinafore: plates of sausage and egg, great heaps of beans, bread, thick cups nearly as big as jam jars full of hot tea, and I couldn't eat anything but I drank some tea, shakily, shivering with cold and strangeness.

It was good going over on the huge boat, amazing, climbing up into it from the quayside, then exploring it gradually, feeling it move, an utterly new sensation. But a terrible cloud descended when we found the field, three miles out of Douglas on the mountain road to Snaefell, right against the T.T. course. The field was as rough and inhospitable as a common, lumpy, with poor coarse grass thick with thistles. My father looked at it and said nothing, my mother tightened her mouth and went to find the farmhouse and see about milk and bread. She met a slobbering imbecile at the door of a filthy kitchen, her left arm withered and useless, hair in rats' tails, broken slippers falling off her feet. She came back to the thistle field, to my father and his lovely old mother, to the Old Sweat, me and my brother. She took one look at the tea chest that was half unpacked, tents and pans and blankets strewn around it pathetically, as if scattered by the wind. She clenched her fists, moaned and burst into tears. My heart broke in me with pity, I felt sick and utterly defeated, bone-poor, and in some awful way homeless and motherless. The only other time I ever felt that way was in the cellar, moving in with our miserable possessions.

A snap of the family on this occasion shows us posed in a Douglas glen, parents staring pensively down at the water in the gloomy light. Standing behind are the sons, both in grey flannel suits, Alan with a plastic camera from Woolworths dangled over his shoulder—against us the white X of the little bridge leaps out. I look tough, one elbow shoved akimbo, arm around Alan's shoulder in an elder brother stance, my mouth full and sulky. Alan looks rounder, cherubic, his nose shorter than mine, but already the face has the in-growing signs, the locked-away life—soon we'll be strangers. My Dad's bespectacled head is dark with thought, he sits brooding in his cheap striped sports shirt, his sports coat and flannels, preoccupied. As well as being on holiday he goes around Douglas during weekdays making mysterious calls on garages, forging business links for his firm, or trying. I never believe, never feel he is making much impression on the business world—even at that age I can sense it. The cannibalistic, fast-thinking, shifty-eyed businessmen are dealing in one currency and him another —and he can't see it. I'm a child, I can see it. He will never, never see it. Not through lack of ability; but he is some kind of misfit. Instead of loving him for it, I want to walk away and leave him, disown him. I feel unsafe. Where he should cut short a conversation he keeps on, and his approach isn't cold and efficient like theirs, machine-like; he halts in the middle of sentences, reminisces, changes direction, meanders, or else rattles on too eagerly. If he is listening, he is sympathetic, curious, ready to stand there all day, full of respect—fatally interested. He can't fake like them, he's no match for them. He thinks he can combine business with being a human being: no, he doesn't think it, he just can't act in any other way. Disastrous. In the photo my mother sits beside this ridiculously human being, her black hair scraped back, forehead puckered, her bony, handsome, gypsyish face gaunt with worry as usual. Perhaps his goodness makes her nervous, even terrifies her at times, as it does me. She stares into the shadows. Under her left arm a handbag, inside which is bound to be her purse. Unrelaxed, she clutches the handbag, hangs on to her worries and responsibilities, holiday or no holiday.

I came to hate and even despise the goodness of my father. It made him weak and comic, it got us trampled on. I had a ruthless period, a young pride and power, a hatred of weakness. Mine most of all. Now the only abiding impression I can give of my old man resurrects this despised goodness. I don't gloss him over, he was no saint. But too good and decent and straightforward in his dealings ever to get on in this world. So he stayed a clerk. An awkward customer for the bosses, the managements, I can imagine— in spite of his eager friendliness and adaptability. Not a rebel, just too honest for his own good. What a fool, stupid, a fool to himself, they must often have said in contempt behind his back. More than once he got sacked because of principles, conscience. There was the Humber story: with lockouts, strikes, pickets on their hands they tried to swear in office staff as works police, even issuing them with guns.

My father refused—and got his notice soon after: a neat little letter arrived while he was on holiday, informing him that his services were no longer required. As a labour exchange clerk in the thirties I can imagine him dealing fair, no little Hitler act, no doling it out grudgingly like a man with no arms. Again, he got nowhere. The whole of his working life it's been the same story.

Those names and faces connected with holidays, the snaps, the snatches of talk and incident, they are woven and interwoven into the very fabric of those times; names like Dennis Kingsbury, Caroline, Harry Bussell, Wal Leavins and Dora . . . faces of paradise. Benign, beaming, oiled with the sun of leisure, laughing. All connected in some way with Geoff, who opened out almost sunnily among them. Open for him, that is. For he belonged to our shy tribe, he always kept something back. Not like his old mate Wal Leavins, or Wal's wife Dora, both of them lovable, wide-open people, unbelievable, too good to be true. I watched them and listened to them and hung on to their words because they were so warm and happy, so wholesome. They fascinated me. And it was true, they really were like that. They glowed with simple happiness, or contentment. I saw them in the best possible circumstances, I know—but holidays or workdays or gloomy Sundays, they always seemed in that state of euphoria. Wal was ginger, fuzzy, a broad honest face covered in a mask of freckles, his voice cracking delightfully as he spoke—you could imagine it breaking down with the sheer weight of heart it carried —and he spoke slowly, quietly, in simple homely accents, screwing up his eyes and laughing every few minutes. He was a town yokel. Listening to his queer croak and looking fearlessly into his face I used to be stirred by an almost voluptuous sensation of happiness myself, and excited too, as if on the verge of a wonderful discovery. There was a tang sometimes in what he said—he was a skilled mechanic at Ferguson's—and he'd glance at Dora in silence while she was holding forth, give her salty, amused, indulgent glances. They were a lovely couple. She was plump, gasping out laughs, had a high excited voice and seemed permanently hot and flustered, and as if embarrassed by her own life, her health and joy. She overflowed with it, for no reason—how did it happen, why should she feel like it? It astonished her, plainly. She went red as a tomato with embarrassment, and Wal would look at her, shake his head, laugh, wrinkle his eyes, rub his freckled cheeks. His big mouth would crack open in a grin. ' Don't ask me,' was a thing he was always saying. ' Don't ask me, Geoff.' ' Don't ask me, Jack.' The talk was often about engine innards, either cars or motorbikes, the breakdowns and accidents and mishaps they'd had, which gave spice and adventure to their journeys : the smooth running performances were prideful, pleasant, but they weren't a patch on misfortunes when it came to holding the interest. This was in the days when to be on the road with your vehicle, coaxing and nursing it, was an adventure, an act of independence, a new freedom. Suddenly you owned land, you swooped over England from town to town and it intoxicated you, the freedom of the open road : you swung round the coasts and found out where you were living and this was real geography, on next to no money. Wal Leavins rode his Norton combination as if he was made of the same material—stamped it heavily into pulsing life and sat back, settling himself like an old aristocrat, or a groom. He'd sit there inert letting it throb under him, stationary, while he listened, a queer stoical abstraction now, his Dora wedged into the sidecar and silenced by the roar, doused by the hood, the celluloid screens. They'd thunder away, powerful rather than fast, bumping and rolling away from us and our camp, over the dry hard field. They'd never stay long : have a look at us for a few hours one afternoon, on their way to relatives or coming back from somewhere. Once or twice they stopped long enough for a swim. They had two kids, little girls, chips off the same laughing contentment, darting through the brown water like minnows. The bike thundered, then chugged and it was them, an amiable vehicle of life, going again. The Leavins'. *Ta-ra! Ta-ra!* We'd watch them until they disappeared.

43

9

It occurs to me that a log of the writing of this book could be stitched into it as it grows, just as those names I mentioned are sewn into the very cloth of my boy's heaven. That's how a book should be, spilling its secrets as it goes. Blabbing, giving the game away. Who believes in a book cut away from its writer with surgical scissors? I don't, I never did. I don't believe in fact and fiction, I don't believe in autobiography, poetry, philosophy, I don't believe in chapters, in a story. Words tell their own story and not the one you intended, ever. The power of words. You can tell the tale of the flesh and waste your time, it's the scar tissue you should have concentrated on. In the end you find out what a prison a book is, no matter how you go at it. If you're opposed to books as prisons, as I used to be—still am, sometimes—you batter against the brick and never get out. That's the queer thing. Once you give up hope, give up external desires, your life turns inward and feeds on what is there. Dreams fill out, expand, bulge through the walls. When they ask you what it's like being locked away for life, you want to laugh. The intensity of your dreams has begun to dominate your existence; the word freedom fades. It belonged with the hard look and the surly mouth of youth, the insolent Rimbaud face, giving the V-sign, blowing a dirty fat raspberry on the back of your hand, showing authority your arse. Before long the word will have misted over and then dropped out of your vocabulary: soon you'll have a struggle to remember what it means. That's the idyllic state and I'm a long way off. What I do, I give myself instructions, orders of the day. As a young clerk working out wages, I used to make entries in red ink with a steel pen. The red ink stained my fingers; I'd wash and scrub at them, and look—it was still there, a faint stain like clerk's blood. I want to write a book like that, in my clerk's blood. In the heart's blood. In a father's blood, a lover's, in a boy's blood. Bull's blood. My mother's blood. A dream in red ink. Blood from the cut artery, straight into the red ledger.

My life so far falls clearly into three sections, each one a prison, the sentences running more or less concurrently, with time out on short paroles. School. Factory. Office. No, not quite as simple as that—nothing is ever that simple. Other conditions, prisons, half prisons, cut in and out of these three; all kinds of shadings, cross-hatchings. Parents. Marriage. Obscurity, and the journey out. The Midlands, then the complete break, the shift to the south of all of us : parents, brother, friend, wife. I seem to be concentrating on the first two sections now, and some paroles. The prison of sex closes in during the office section, which I am still in, and when I've served my sentence there and come out I intend to deal with that. It may prove the richest in terms of points of departure, turning points, seeing a pattern emerge. Then the war should be coming to an end, fires banked : time to marry the whole thing together and see what issues, what kind of human family. Who's got piles, who belches and suffers from heartburn, who needs an operation for gallstones. Count the casualties and add up the winnings. Or maybe not like that at all—it's all too far away. When I think of the wounds and how they open without warning, the terrible sudden rages, exasperation, melancholia, choking fits—no, I can't imagine how it will end, not yet. So many unforeseen developments, surprises —that's life.

Who'd have dreamt, for instance, that I'd be so thick with a young blood twenty years younger than me—a car fiend? He's solid, stocky, blond curls, good-looking in a pug-nosed, pouting way : a real-life child of this age. A comedy fan, and that's what redeems him for me, that and his young kicking trapped life, his dirtied-up inno-cence. This century produced him and he jeers at every-thing in it, because he feels the phoney and the flash on his veins. The only thing worse than the cheating present is the dead hand of the past. He picks up an old glass ink-well, grips it in his hand like a grenade, grits his teeth and says, ' Christ, look at it—I hate anything like this. I do, I want to smash it—gives me the creeps.' He feels the same way about Dickens, about old anything. It traps him,

chokes and drags, holds him back. I'm attracted to him by
his goon humour, and by his contempt for guff, regulation
and discipline—like most of his generation he's already left
traditional England behind. When the boss gave him a
playful cuff on the head for cheek, only a fortnight after
Tommy had started, I heard ' Keep your hands off !' and
looked up to see a bunched fist, the boss jerking back as if
stung. I shivered with delight, hoping for more ferocity.
Nothing doing : he's afraid his temper will expose him to
ridicule. Now, if he's reprimanded like a schoolboy, he gets
up with his face dark and goes out, slamming the door. The
boss loathes him with the full force of his scrat-and-save
soul, the whole span of his skin-and-grief years. Can't
accept the inevitable, can't hear the death rattle of his day
and age : he still expects respect. Doesn't he know the Time
of the Hooligans is upon us? Tommy gives him the raspberry, loud and clear. It's mutual. The job is a means to
an end for Tommy, with no pretence of worry or conscien-
tiousness. He couldn't care less how a member of the staff
is supposed to behave; at knocking-off time he makes for
the door in one bound like a Ford worker. He's restless,
empty, itching about for something to kill time. I cultivate
his comic side as hard as I can go because then he flowers :
we join forces, mimic, take the piss, and all anybody can
complain of is our giggling. I know that basically he's
sterile, deprived, wasted, and nobody is ever going to make
use of his heroic qualities. The way he hurls himself around,
leaps down staircases, lets his hair grow until it curls over
his collar, then crops it off short angrily—these are pointless, beautiful gestures like his car driving. His projectile-
like nature longs for a target : all he can find is marriage,
and how it makes him writhe, the thought of it. He orders
a suit for the day, decorates a flat, meets his girl every
day, every night, every week-end. He's bored. Marriage
won't fit him, he suspects—not his style. He'll be in the
clutches then like all the others. What is his style? Ask
him and he'll shrug, grin, pull down his cruel little mouth,
hunch over the wheel and drive faster. He doesn't care for
those direct questions. ' Jesus, I'm depressed !' he'll howl,
too savage for laughs.

The open exhaust sounds like a plane dive-bombing the town centre. He drives too fast, with marvellous sham indifference. A power kid, born to it. Starting off, he drops into position as if into a cockpit. Slams the door, reaches immediately for the car radio under the dashboard. Distorted music crackles out, a jangly beat: the Light. The Mini tears off, the exhaust adds its yell to the singer's, the wheels contribute a separate, more dangerous rhythm. Tommy's eyes take on a drugged, sent, wall-eyed look. The change is physical, as the power runs into him, and it can happen a thousand times and I'll still find it uncanny. Belting down the straight, driving with the soles of his feet and just one hand that he lets droop on the vibrating wheel as if by accident, he lolls sideways against the offside door. Moodily he watches the road, lunges up savagely to rub at the smeared windscreen with the sleeve of his flying jacket, slumps back, swings in behind the tail of a lorry, suddenly snarls out violently, 'Come arn!' It's strange, all his attractive humour submerges when he gets in the car. His gravity, arrogance, masterful firmness join to explode him through the traffic in male assertion. When his girl gets in she is meek, submissive, and if he bothers to speak at all it's curtly, even brutally. King of the road, this is his kingdom. And she doesn't object to this neglect; her turn comes later. Ramming up through a side street he sees a hairy beatnik on the pavement. He yanks furiously at the window handle to wind down the glass, then bawls out 'Scruff!' as he rips past. Canada attracts him—his sister lives at Toronto—but his roots are his parents, his girl, her parents, the pub: he senses this resentfully. He is still after all English and rooted, not the world projectile he favours. Give him time, he could be, but he hasn't been anywhere yet. He's temporary: job, flat, car, country, everything is for the time being. I hope he doesn't leave yet or go abroad, I like him more and more. It's only in the car that I lose contact with him, when he ceases to be human. He's a killer then, I feel. His negative attitudes are sound enough. Routines, forms, politics, they're just 'cokernuts'. He drinks at the Embassy Club, the Astoria, the London Inn, and when he goes to bed he throws off his clothes and

sleeps ' horny '. The class line cuts at him, same as everywhere in little England, and he reacts bitterly : jeers, sets
his head uglily, but soon recovers his good humour. If he
says a word wrong, or misspells, he blushes and loses his
fine youthful swagger. Then I loathe England, good and
proper. It seems crawling with shits. Ashamed, I bend over
backwards to put him at his ease again. Nothing confuses
him easier than class. He lives in a prefab and insults the
tabloids, takes an occasional *Times*, then Sunday finds him
with the *News of the World*. Girlie magazines are jammed
in his car pockets. He's fine, he suits me. I steer us both
through the day as cutely as he steers me through the town,
only my driving is sly, unimpressive, and for different
reasons. I drive to keep us travelling. If he leaves I shall be
back in the graveyard with my thoughts. I work like a
jester to keep him bobbing like a cork.

He doesn't even remember the war, though of course it's
been dinned into him, and he grew up seeing the ruins,
bomb sites, having the scars pointed out to him. That and
war films, pulp stories, TV documentaries. Inside his car
it's sluttish, like his desk, but he has no time for poverty.
Hire purchase is second nature to him. The only way he
can keep money is by handing it over to his girl or his
mother. If a thing's dilapidated his instinct is to chuck it
in the dustbin. He was driving his own Consul at seventeen,
paying back the loan by instalments. If I could take him
back to my childhood in Ernaldlhay Street, decent and
respectable slum, I bet he'd turn up his nose.

Ernaldlhay Street—how did it get a name like that? If
anybody asked you where you lived, you had to say it and
then you were forced to spell it. Always.

And the other names, key names of the Street : Albey's,
Miss Eames, the Macadams, the Shuters, Waterhouse's
shop, Black's shop. The Eagle, St Stephen's School, the
Parochial Rooms. Miller's newspaper shop on the Hyson
Road corner—real name Müller, he changed it at the beginning of the first world war because of the hostility towards Germans. On the opposite corner to him, a garage,
Scanlon's, then up that direction, towards the park, was
another paper shop and a barber's, all belonging to Mr

Miller, who seemed to use the shop next to the barber's as his headquarters. Though it may have been that he was there so much because once in he couldn't get out again without a lot of trouble. The shopkeeper was short, bullet-headed, and the counter came up to his chin, so that he looked embedded in papers, magazines, boxes of chocolates and cartons of cigarettes, as well as a mass of miscellaneous junk such as stationery, doilys, serviettes, trashy pens and pencils.

At the back of the house, down the entry, the huge sinister block of the old Humber factory filled the sky, its grim red brick covered in zigzagging black fire escapes. As a boy I accepted without question this hideous backdrop —and now I come to think of it there *was* something theatrical and cardboard-like about it—just as I would have taken for granted a rolling landscape of lush fields and leafy trees. Between this gruesome vision and the slimy greenish wood of the entry fence was a dairy, steaming and rattling day and night. The cardboard tops of the used milk bottles were dumped against the fence, their undersides encrusted with sour milk. These mouldy discs were great for spinning, so we used to squeeze through gaps in the boards and grab handfuls. If you couldn't see any mounds, you just made for the smell.

The street was a link between two arteries, Hyson Road and Whatford Street. Taken on its own it was absolutely nondescript, just a slot between two rows of identical ter-raced houses with the front doors flush to the pavement; all exactly alike at first glance, even to the paintwork. You had to belong to the street to notice the differences. Mrs Stanley's net curtains sagged, and they got blacker and blacker, a disgrace to the street, hanging there shamelessly like tatters of dirty bandage: Mrs McCollam's was the one that had a whiff of coal gas clinging to it; the smell seeped under the front door, and if you had to knock and go in for shillings for the meter it nearly gassed you, in her kitchen. That gash in the wall under Slater's front window was where a van skidded and ran off the road.

Whatford Street was where the blood poured, especially Saturdays, because it went straight uphill to the Town, the

shops, the market. And it was a street of shops in itself :
shops, pubs, pictures, chapel, the great gloomy cliff of the
Humber flanking it near the bottom of the hill. Hyson Hill
had none of this character, nothing to gawp at—just a road
for getting somewhere. It climbed up past the hospital and
at the top where the workhouse stood on the corner it
joined the main London road. We were always being
warned about that, to watch out for the lorries. Heard
grisly tales of accidents, a man on a bike dragged a hundred yards under a heavy lorry up there one winter's night,
and when they got him out he had no legs, one arm . . .
It was the way out to the big world, a vague meaningless
place at the other end. We only knew it as the route to the
Common, to Warmeleigh, to Sutton Aerodrome and Alvington and the Abbey. There was another link I came to
know between these two arteries, really an alleyway between high factory walls and warehouses, no more than a
slit, called Shut Lane. It filled me with a creepy feeling,
half dread and half fascination. I used to start walking
through it and end up by running madly in a panic. At
the Hyson Road entrance was a stadium they used for all-
in wrestling, and it came out in Whatford Street by the
high railings of a monumental mason. It ought to have
been called Shit Lane—there was dog shit everywhere. The
bricks were decorated with chalk drawings of cocks and
tits, there was the odd splash of vomit and the puddles of
piss left by drunks turned out of pubs the night before.

Amazing how you kept to your own district as if you
lived in a village; clung to it like a mother, hurried back to
it fearfully when you were in trouble. And if you pene-
trated other districts, say in the company of your Grandpa,
how the strangeness made you blink, how it chilled you,
made you suffer. The Ford Street, Alma Road area was
adjacent to ours, but subtly different, dominated by the
B.T.H. factory as ours was overshadowed by the Humber
building. East Street, Waterloo Street, Wellington Street,
Broad Street, Springfield Road, Vernon Street and all the
slums making Greenfields were different in another, more
oppressive and menacing way—the entries tunnel-like,
often cobbled, with common taps in the backs and lava-

tories in blocks of four, and ashy bits of dirt like poultry
runs for gardens. Our streets were jammed tight with the
same pinched and meagre dwellings, the people in them
shared the same kind of life and hard times, but somehow
the bricks didn't seem to have that harsh, north-bitten in-
dustrial look: not quite, not to the same extent. Yet they
bordered on it, one side, while the other side trailed off into
a pattern of streets with bits of trim front garden, and
further on still the bay windows, till you were amongst the
semis and garages and wrought-iron gates of Acacia
Avenue and Harper Road. The thick walls of privet, the
cropped lawns, glossy woodwork. Going through this clean,
dead and snotty world was one way of getting to the
Common—past the cemetery and the Stilbrook tucked
away behind, down the London Road where the lorries
batted, under the bridge, and suddenly it opened out, a
scrubby no-man's land, with its gorse bushes and crab-
apples and paths where the grass had worn bald, the clayey
hummocks and pits free to anybody, no fences, no signs, no
park keeper. You wanted to run and roll about and lie
down, it was so exciting. There were secret hideouts in the
jungle of thickets, among the stunted oaks and alder
bushes—that was where Roy Turnbull took us one Saturday morning, unfastened his belt and showed us his hard
bent prick—bent like a bow. It was thin and shiny and
mean-looking, but the ugliest thing about it was the way
it curved. I took an instant dislike to it.

Long before that, a gang of us took a girl up the concrete sewer which tunnelled into the bank of the Willey—
at the edge of the cindery waste-piece where the fair came
every Bank Holiday. Somebody had a candle. We didn't
go far down the pipe, it looked black as hell and we got
frightened, even though we could still see the rim of daylight. She had her knickers off, ready. ' Let's see then,' our
leader said, the oldest. She started to whimper, frightened
of the dark. Somebody lit the stump of candle. She lifted
up her dress round her grubby belly just long enough for
us to stare in disbelief at her little cunt. ' I want to go
home,' she whimpered. We all scrambled out, split up. I
got a good hiding for getting my feet wet.

10

THE story of my playmates has to begin with Desmond Brockway, the boy with the round felt hat like a girl's, the only boy who was ever frightened of me. First I chased him, then I befriended him on that first day of school. I chased him because of his hat, that's all; because it was a grey colour, and round, unusual, and I felt an urge to touch it. He cowered in a corner, panting, and I smiled at him, reached out and touched his hat. It dawned on him that I wasn't going to hurt him. I can see him even now, his soft spoiled mouth and those brown, not quite sincere eyes. Staring and pouting, fraternising, ready to run, make a bolt for it if I changed my mind and turned nasty. He was like that, expedient, even at the age of five. Maybe he's a successful politician now. His father had a furniture shop, he was well off by our standards. You only had to look at Desmond's clothes. He was an only child. He took me home to play a few times, up in the big room over the shop where they lived. It was warm, luxurious, spacious, a soft-carpeted world stocked with expensive toys, anything Desmond wanted. He lolled on the floor, heaps of toys and books strewn about, bored and spoiled. Over the road, nearly opposite, was the hovel where Doris Platt lived, a snot-nosed ragged kid in our class. Her father had a tiny greengrocer's shop right under the shadow of the Humber, and it was like a cave, the rough walls running with damp. It stank of mildew and poverty in there. The low ceiling bulged down ominously over the window, and on the blotchy walls he'd nailed square paintings he'd done himself on the lids of cardboard boxes. They were lurid pictures, a lopsided child's vision of the world, but with the innocence gone rancid and sickly, like the smell in his shop. Portraits there were, big swollen noses and heavy jaws, and several versions of a swan on a stagnant, acid-green pool. He had the same pockmarked, bulbous nose as his painted heads, and he came shuffling in from the back in his brown cow-gown, peering through his round steel glasses.

Well, no, he didn't exactly peer—he didn't anything. He was extinct, dead on his feet. His dirty yellowy-white hair looked unhealthy, and it was plastered down over the bald patches. He was pitiful, and he was a meek loony, so you weren't sorry so much as scared. He was queer, he belonged to another species, and you didn't waste pity on him because he was beyond pity, beyond hope, beyond everything. It was so obvious that he was out of reach, in another world. All the kids were scared of his blank look and his seized-up Frankenstein neck; they found him creepy, though it's true he didn't do anything. And that was what vaguely terrified; his silence, which nobody made any attempt to bridge. It was like a foreigner—nobody knew the language or bothered to learn it, or imagined they were capable of the same feelings as other people; they were on a different circuit. Old Platt was so far off he might have been on another planet—an extinct one. He'd shamble out of his hole from the living quarters in the back and stand at his counter—it was more like a fence. He stood there, dumb, cut off at the waist, legless, his face fixed in a permanent faint smile of weary hopelessness. It wasn't really an expression, it was eaten into his face, encrusted. The glasses magnified his eyes, blurring and distorting the iris into a huge grey oval swimming in sadness, so that he looked blind, waiting and listening for something to happen. No please or thank you—when you were served he turned like a sheep and trundled back through the hole in the wall again, an opening hardly big enough for him to push through. Perhaps he was engrossed in some picture he was painting and wanted to get back to it. Perhaps . . . but he had this sinister quality.

Poor Doris Platt stank, the stink reminded you of Platt's fetid little shop, and she was simple in the head. She sat in the classroom liking everybody, smiling round at everything, a gentle thing like a saint, as idiots are sometimes in this world. There was a woman I used to see who lived tucked away in a back street somewhere in the district who was half blind, and half off her rocker, fumbling round the corner at the same hour each day, taking her mongrel for a walk, and she'd catch sight of you dimly through her glasses and the smile would break on her face spontaneously, welling up from deep inside and reaching her face and flowering. Dorothy might have ended like that. She wore round steel glasses, like her old man. She must have been six or seven, no more; a lovely age. Completely oblivious of her ripped clothes and broken shoes.

It's true I didn't see any of it like this, I couldn't have done—how could I? I was living it, breathing it in and out, and on Saturdays in bustling Whatford Street I dodged prams, shoppers, mingling with the parade. The whole ugly shitheap was my homely romping ground: no judgements were being passed on any of it, I had no values or standards. Wherever it marked me, wounded me, it left scars of paradise. I know I'll never get back there, though I dream of it. I nearly described it once as a time of piercing sweetness, but that's wrong; it's only now when it's too late that it pierces, and I suppose that's the purity. Then it was simply wonderful, a wonderful enveloping sweetness, a delicious terror. As a boy of five I sat in the strange room called a classroom, quivering at the separation, torn away from home, from my mother—she was only at the other end of the street but it could have been the other side of the world. I gazed in wonder at the teacher, Miss Warren, behind her a slide of pale yellow wood to be used on wet days, and I noticed the boy to the left of me, his bare knees scratched and scabby. I saw the posies of wild flowers arranged in jam jars on the windowsills, limp fountains of wilting bluebells, the crayon pictures tacked up on the walls. We sang *Away in a Manger*, we made marks on squared paper, I chased the boy in the felt hat with the brim to it, and ran home at twelve to tell my mother.

The boy on my left was Steve Mallard: the name is heroic. I kept my pencils and rubber in a cardboard box that had been used for Woodbines—it was still pungent with the smell of tobacco. Tiny grains were lodged in the corners. I may have asked for the box at the tobacconist's across the street—' Please can I have an empty box, Mister ' —or they may have given it to me at home, or perhaps the teacher did, I can't remember. Later on, older and tougher already, we'd race round the corner to the cake shop before nine, asking for stale cakes and broken biscuits. For tuppence you could get a bagful of buns and rock cakes a day or two old, if you were lucky. A little queue of kids would be bundled in there most mornings, panting from the run after hurling themselves at the door to get in first, a smoke of breath coming out of their mouths if it was frosty.

If I had the power and could relive it again, one tiny occasion would be sufficient to recapture the joy and bliss, the thrilling tenderness of those days, when nothing more than a sensation of wonder made you so happy, so rapt. We were in the Parochial Rooms, a rambling building of dusty bare rooms which belonged to the church, used by the school for concerts, and by other groups who organised lantern lectures, cinematograph shows—I saw the Charlie Chaplin silents there, itching about painfully on the hard wooden seats, craning my neck, groaning in anguish when the film snapped. But the moment of bliss, longed for ever since—maybe it's a dream—came one December morning in a top room of this building. It was a rehearsal for our Christmas concert. There was the wonder and mystery of being there at all during school time, and smelling the dust, and the paper chains were up, hanging over the lights, draping the doorway. One of my classmates was on the stage, piping up in his fresh beautiful voice, and it might have been ' Little Old Lady' or something atrocious like that he was singing. I had nothing to do, no part, no worry, it was a beautiful song to me and I loved him, loved the scene, the quality of the daylight, so grey it hardly entered the window, the time of the morning, the nearness to Christmas and the marvellous signs of it, tokens of delight, the paper chains, the red crêpe paper pinned along the front edge of the platform. I was so fused and in harmony with it all, I even loved the creak of the bare boards as the singer moved his feet nervously, and the way our high voices echoed in the big cold space.

True bliss. Like the Friday afternoons on the eve of breaking-up time, and they allowed you to bring your own books, even games, and as long as you kept quiet it was all right to change seats and go and sit beside your best friend, reading the same page of the same book with heads together, whispering 'Have you finished? Read it yet? Can I turn over now?' Like being given a special job out-side, quite suddenly out of the blue, a pure gift from heaven—'Go and weed in front of the Headmaster's office.' Going out quietly with heart pounding, actually out in the open street, to the narrow strip of cobbles under His Window—you could even hear him rustling papers in there, hear his chair scrape as you stooped down under the windowsill, crouched on your heels and tugged at the grass tufts, dug with a stick or your fingernails at the ribs of soft moss. Like the journey through the streets with the wicker linen basket full of fresh eggs which the whole school had collected to give to the hospital—yours among them somewhere, wheedled out of your mother's pantry—and a white cloth over the eggs, you on one handle and a boy you didn't like much on the other, to help carry this cargo dangerous as dynamite, walking very gingerly so as not to stumble, feeling happier with every step and soon liking the boy better. 'Want to change sides?' And you liked the thought of the hospital drawing nearer, the jour-ney more pleasurable and less terrifying as you dwelt on that and on the return trip with nothing, absolutely nothing to worry about, just an empty basket you could swing and let drop and even wear like a huge hat if there was a shower of rain.

11

WE tore up the roots and left the city, as if for good. We lived through the war, chained to the city by jobs, relatives. I didn't visit the old district once, it was submerged and lost, gone for ever as far as I was concerned. But there was no place for us in Lillington, no real home I suppose. We were like refugees, visitors, and though it didn't matter to me in the least, infected with the truly modern rootlessness, it did matter to my mother, born in St John Street with the church spires on her horizon. It may have mattered to my father too, but he was adaptable, he welcomed change.

It would be my mother, sensitive to atmospheres, feeling unwanted, homesick for the familiar, timid and stubborn and morose, she would be the driving force to get back to the old ground. I was too young to be in on the move, but my father always gave an impression of contentment, compared to my mother, who presented a suffering face: she struggled, put up with it, made the best of a bad job. Of the two, my father was undoubtedly the brightest, the one who shed light. He was blithe, abstracted. If he was suffering and making sacrifices, you weren't made aware of the fact. My mother had gone without food for us in the twenties, pushing the pram through the park in Leicester—where they lived in rooms for a while—feeling sick and faint, and long before I was told this I felt it. She was dark with sacrifice, burdened with love for us. We piled burdens on her willingly, remorseful now and then: if she didn't want us to, why didn't she stop us? Because she loved us too much. Because it all helped to bind us to her. When the weight of this love began to make us heavy with guilt, being sons we were soon kicking and longing to leave, yet afraid. Weak with love as we were, attenuated like that, the world frightened us half to death. The old, old story of sons in England, coddled and comforted by the mother who yearns over them like a lover, all sacrificial, till the spunk's sucked out of them. It nearly happened, nearly.

Back in the city after the war, in a nice clean modern district of semi-detached, gravel, front gates, the groves and avenues of suburbia, I went once deliberately down into town, plunging downhill on my bike past the Odeon into the dirty old district of those days, in a deliberate, vaguely desperate attempt to retrace my lost steps. I found the Street horribly shrunken and commonplace, not a shred of the glamour I'd dreamed of, and the Parochial Rooms, that hall of radiance, I almost passed it without noticing it, it was so tatty and inconspicuous and small. Small, everything small. No majesty. I even walked by the house itself, peered up the entry, and it was meaningless, utterly dead. I haven't been back there since. The only way I can go back, richly, truly, is in imagination. I had to learn, I wasn't to know that then. That was why, soon afterwards when I started to write about it in the first book I ever attempted, at the tender age of twenty-one, it was such a howling disaster. The war was over, we were back and installed in a bombed and rebuilt semi-detached at Bloomfield Grove—not streets, they were sunk in the past—and it was the quiet bottle-end of a short cul-de-sac, very new and suburban, near the Birmingham Road. I had a box-room to myself and a typewriter, an old office machine, table under the window—perfect conditions. I wanted to build something up, mine, to set against the factory, against school, against destruction, against my own inadequacy most of all. My father downstairs under my feet—I was screaming at him now inside and he got the message. Once or twice I blurted out my raging intolerance of the whole works, and, of course, it implicated him as an Elder, included him, because he was of it and took it for granted.

' You silly twerp,' he jeered.

' Open the prisons,' I yelled, my face on fire. ' What's everybody afraid of?' I fell into incoherence, I was easy meat. Even my mother joined in the game, chopping me to pieces with the same dull logic my father used, and she laughed indulgently. So I sat in my cell nursing this terrible desire to build, build something, for God's sake. Get me out of this. Build out of nothing, no experience, build by wanting to build urgently enough. Tear down their lies and hypocrisy, set fire to their churches and treadmills and sheep-pens and slaughterhouses. A clean start. Let them keep away from me—their very talk stinks up the place. Let them fight their own dirty wars, I was on my way out, on my own. Then I was face to face with the awful question: What are you going to build? What with? I'd made stories and poems, but they weren't nearly solid and substantial enough. A book was. It was a complete thing like a building, with its own foundations and plumbing. You used words like bricks, steadily and methodically like a bricklayer, one on top of the other: long straight lines, and the building rose, it was yours.

So I sat at the rickety table with a pile of crisp clean paper beside me, lovely. They thought I was all set to be harnessed to a lifetime of honest grafting, did they, just like them? Hard graft was the banner of their religion. Work was their God, I knew that, it had been hammered into me by example, and into them by their parents, and so on—right back to Carlyle. You could tell them God was a fairy tale, Jesus wasn't important like electricity, and they'd smile or go deaf. They weren't upset, or not deeply, and it certainly didn't worry them. My mother was ' religious ', but not if it interfered with the *important* duties, such as housework. She was too busy to go to church anyway—and as a child she was conscripted into bible classes, Sunday school, church services three times a day on the Sabbath, evangelist tent meetings, mission work, Sunshine Leagues—enough to last her for the rest of her life, you'd think. No wonder she was ' religious ' and felt she could afford to smile away my foolishness. My father had nothing whatever to say on the subject of religion. I think he kept quiet, hoping it would go away. But if you blasphemed against work, a great wail went up from your mother. Your father went for you viciously, pulverised you with contempt —' You little twerp, wipe your chin it's dribbling !' Or he gave you the blah blah about learning by experience, like an old goat. ' We had to fight for it, son, the right to work. Yes you can laugh—you'll find out.'

I did. But then I hadn't, and I wasn't going to, either. I chewed my lips, gulped, swallowed down my pride. I was about to go off like a lightning flash—what were they talking such drivel to me for? Did they know what was happening inside me, like a feast of blossom opening on a bush in the night? Well, perhaps they were being a little hasty. He's young, he's hot-headed, he hasn't even got the cradle marks off his behind yet, give him time and he'll find out and calm down, all by himself. We all go through the same phase. Let him paint and write and listen to records and act funny, mooning around in the front room every week-end, jabbing at the piano—it's nice to have hobbies. He'll come round : let it dribble off his chin for a while. I suppose he gets his daft ideas out of books : still never mind, you can't stop him reading. Education's a wonderful thing, gets you a good job. They used to try so hard to be understanding, it was pitiful sometimes—until I stuck my foot in it again, that great arsehole of creation they called Work and Money. You've got to have money, son, in this world. I'd try to stop it but no good, it'd jerk out, boiling hot: Why have you? Then they went nuts. Their platitudes caught alight, real passion at last; it was guaranteed. In the end they did their best to ignore me, let me go my own way, so that instead of having the luxury of hating them I felt nauseated by my own selfishness and stiff-necked pride. They'd been good to me and they were still good; that's where they always had you. You hated them for that most of all, like a man hates his creditors.

I sat up there in awful isolation, in a labyrinth of quiet avenues like the cemetery along the Birmingham Road. I was sickly with mother-love, a lovekin, even though I'd been blooded at the big school and the factory. I still trembled on the threshold. Why didn't they understand, when I dashed their hopes and rejected their beliefs, stamped on their fears, that the most savage revolt wasn't against them but going on inside me? They couldn't understand, no matter how deep their understanding, because I was on my own plot of land, my own kingdom, tearing down and dreaming and longing to build, and I was the only one with the key.

I wrote the book, sweated blood over its lousy pages, squeezed it out agonisingly, sentence by sentence, word by word. What I had in the end was terrible judgement on me: a heap of waste paper, dead feeling; an abortion. What killed it more than anything was my timidity. A voice inside me was demanding real facts, real names, even then. I didn't have the guts to listen, but even at this early stage I had an instinctive distrust of made-up stuff, fiction. I should have taken a pride in the place, made the people say ta and oh ah and our kid and any road, filled it with place names like Lob End and Cannon Street and Whitelake. Instead I took refuge in the notion that you needed a style for writing, and if you didn't have one you had to find one from somewhere; graft it on. English writers hardly existed in my world, they were a class apart, right out of it with their noses in the air. I turned over Faulkner, Hemingway—at least they had a living, warm quality. But

I ended up with their styles and that was fatal. I needed something native to nourish me. The whole clue to me and what I wanted to say was in my Englishness. I was for ever peering at other books, seeing how other writers put things —I was like an art student trying to discover the secrets of perspective, light and shade, how to convey the illusion of a third dimension. How to make a nose stick out so that you can almost grab hold of it, how to make an eyeball look round and solid like a marble. And basically, bitterly, I had nothing to say anyway; no real impetus to carry me through a book. I wanted to build something, so why not a book? It was purely symbolic, a crutch to lean on and lash out with. Not surprisingly I did a thoroughly pastiche job, a patchwork quilt of my admirations. It grew so painfully, forcing, forcing, that I used to go to the library and stand there pulling out novel after novel in desperation, looking for the least number of pages I needed to be able to call my thing a book. Somehow I finished it—a testament to the very donkey work I despised—that and the ferocity of my will. Long before it was made I loathed it; it was so obviously hybrid and wrong. I was too ashamed to show it to anybody. It got buried at the back of a drawer, a miscarriage. Wrap it in newspaper quick, flush it down the lav. I know now that years of life have to roll through you, and then perhaps you can hit the right note. The tone is everything, the style nothing. If a sentence ever comes out stylish, my instinct is to straightway put kinks in it, make it angular, or anyway a little bent. Then it comes alive. It's queer. If you want to draw the sun, Renoir or somebody said, throw away your compasses. Perfection deadens. I struggled and failed, and struggled again. Nothing there. Empty. A nonentity. Nobody could have helped me, and what sort of advice would it have been if they had, telling me to wait and live a bit? I fairly seethed with impatience. Now I've learned to be tolerant and I tell myself I don't have to hurry: I'm alive, I've survived, they haven't dropped the Bomb yet, it's suspended or stuck up there— but I hurry just the same. That's the age we live in. I'm hurrying now.

So I wrote at another book and put the pages in a file

marked 'London', and this was going to convey the meagre three weeks of the London experience. I made it strong out of weakness, using the raw, naïve, sawn-off sentences of the iconoclast. And called it 'The Dream' because of how it developed, hypnotic, sweated-out, livid as a bad dream . . . 'He unfastened the suitcase and began to get things out. He felt pleased with himself. He was making a new start. He had taken a giant stride. Now he was in a different stream. He would drift along for a bit and see what happened. So this was London! He could hardly believe it. It could be anywhere, there must be rooms like this all over the world, he thought. London! Anything could happen, anything. It was such a vast place, teeming with people of all nationalities. He was very pleased with himself. He had done it. Won. He felt as though he wanted to give a shout of triumph. Instead he slammed his right fist into the pillow, to release the great force within him. He struck it again with all his strength. He didn't see a pillow but a face he had hated all his life . . .' Further on with it, I deleted 'Dream' and wrote 'Vortex', and the story opened with a train, ruthless engine of decision, hurling me into the capital punishment, the vortex—life. I was the bound and gagged neurotic: this was my last chance. I was off to the whirl, the wheel, the centre, hub and arse-hole of civilisation, in a natty Weaver to Wearer blue serge suit, a trench coat with plastic-leather buttons, military epaulettes, and a cardboard case full of underwear and socks, held together by tin clasps, locks and hinges. Timid, quaking, loveless little man, stepping off the train and sniffing it: Euston, that huge porch over the threshold of London. Stepping out fearfully under the soot and zoom of those lacy iron arches, under fluttering pigeons, gloomy light, in a medley of yells, whistles, taxi hoots. The barber's half-way down the steps to the underground lavatories; side-stepping the man with the mop and bucket. The past bearing down on my shoulders in that clanging, echoing great shed. Dizzy, drunk, stupefied already at the thought of it, the enormous scurrying life waiting outside—what that meant in terms of freedom for an absolute nonentity like me.

62

I thought you had to have a theme. I thought you had to sit there grimly, deadly serious, and hammer through to a conclusion. Nobody told me there are no conclusions, it continues, nothing matters, it's just you and nobody else, and if you can't write then write about not being able to . . . Write about something fantastic like throwing money in the fire, like Dostoevsky. I read him in those fat editions in red and cream jackets, the Constance Garnett translations, and they were a bit antiquated and out of focus, as translations often are, but it doesn't matter a damn with Dostoevsky. He gave me splitting headaches, neuralgia, my eyes seemed to be popping out of my skull, I felt like a bedbug and I was dizzy and sick. When I got up and walked out of the room my knees sagged. I had a pal who was reading him at the same time, we'd exchange books and compare notes, or, to be more exact, look at each other and laugh. Because it was so daft and funny and fantastic, being plunged at such an early age into this world of furious suffering and love, our minds pushing out and expanding like mad, coming out of each book in a daze, shell-shocked, and not budging from the streets we lived in and nobody knowing but us.

' How d'you feel after that one?'

' Shattered !'

He didn't affect my writing in the slightest, this Dostoevsky, that was the strange thing. What I was writing, quiet, simple and restrained, a book based on my childhood, wasn't touched by his crazy characters jumping about and flapping their hands, falling down in fits and all the rest of it in those agitated pages. It left me feverish, yes, but where was the connection with my little English life? I couldn't see any. Yet my models were out of touch, utterly, compared with this mad Russian. He was the modern I should have imitated, and I wouldn't have been infected with a false style either, because he hasn't got one. He's slovenly, prolix, a talker more than a writer, littering everywhere with cliches. Still it gets across, factual and fantastic in one breath, the way we are and the way we're going. The raw Slavic force of the Russian is what puts you off and deludes you into thinking it can't apply here—that

63

kind of blind creativity has been left far behind now. Well, it's coming round again : jump on and ride.

I wasn't far enough away from childhood either to describe it. For one thing I was still living at home, joined on. But I'd read *Stephen Hero* and it had done for me. Now I wanted to write mine as if looking through the eyes of a child. That's fake, fiction. Nobody ever returns to that state, they only long for it. The earliest days of my childhood were so serene, harmonious, untroubled, it was like Mozart only better—the only pure happiness I can remember. As soon as passion began, passionate longings, pain and loneliness became the order of the day. Then it was paradise lost : even the bursts of happiness would be bittersweet reminders of how it used to be always, in that unbroken morning of life.

12

PAIN and loneliness, heartaching confusion, enemies who love you. It had a funny side too, if you weren't too intense. Only you were always intense. You crackled with intensity, fears, worries. Knee joints seizing up—Christ, no, not chronic rheumatism at my age, I haven't lived yet. Don't say haven't shagged a woman yet, because it would have made me wince in those days. I was longing to simply put my arms round a girl and pour out love. My chest throbbed with loving tenderness. One day I couldn't stand the pain any longer. Driven to it, I sent in my name and address to a Lonely Hearts club I'd spotted in a woman's magazine—probably my mother's. That would have been appropriate. Such a relief and excitement when the letters came through the front door. I walked in from work as usual one night and my mother handed the packet to me without a word; perhaps a little barely perceptible tightening of the lips, a sign I knew so well. It meant : You have wounded me deeply but I shall never tell. You will never know how you made me suffer. Poor mute mother. I want to snatch the letters and run off, out of her sight. Or shout—'This is it, I'm in touch with the outer world!' I do neither, just walk off quietly as though nothing has happened, letting the packet dangle in my fingers. No importance. Stuff them in my pocket as soon as I'm up the stairs and make a dive for the toilet, the one truly private place in the house. Shove the bolt across in a quiver of exultation and open the first envelope with shaking fingers.

The first one was from a young fellow—how did I come to get that?—who lived in Liverpool and was suffering from a kind of creeping paralysis. He wanted a pen friend, he'd be more than glad to hear from me and he promised to keep writing faithfully as long as he could hold a pen, until his disease reached his fingers . . . I sat down on the lavatory seat, all the stuffing knocked out of me. He sounded so chirpy, God knows why. I stared at his childish, painfully-wobbling scrawl—the last sentence nose-dived into a corner, righted itself, fell backwards, stumbled on again to sign off in a name I couldn't decipher. Yours sincerely. I shut it away, slid it back in the envelope. I didn't want to know. Knock again, nobody at home here, try next door. No thanks—not today. Feeling sick and sad and frightened I opened the next one—a girl, an art student living outside Leeds. All right, but nothing, just how d'you do and would you like to correspond with me. I'd be delighted if you would—but not sounding it. Cool and firm, strapped in tight, a real nice English handshake, frosty. The last thing I wanted. The third letter, warm and sentimental and a bit simple, was from a lonely girl who lived with her widowed mother, worked in an office, comptometer operator, liked to read books and poetry and go for long walks in the country with a dog—it was the only one left and I clutched at it. Desperation works wonders, blinds you even better than love. It was half-witted I suppose, no need to read it twice—it was wet as a scrubber. I seized on it. Humble, good—I pressed virtues into its meek and sloppy sentiments. Who the hell wanted brains, some icy clever-dick? I rushed into the box-room and scribbled a reply there and then to Edwina—that was her name, believe it or not. Her address was Holmanthorpe, Huddersfield, Yorks. Meant nothing to me. I wrote back innocently and brightly, with a touch of fervour, just a touch, and a sort of brotherly warmth, so as not to scare her off. Kept everything out of it except the simple need to alleviate the pain of loneliness which hers betrayed. Only hers was her own, and I was terrified of being myself. I copied her style, cunningly insinuated myself into those half-baked phrases and trotted them out again, like an echo. Next day I wrote to the art student—may as well see if there was anything doing, get a photo at least—and that was different altogether. Jaunty, smart, provocative, the kind of thing I felt she was expecting. Entertainment. The one from the poor crippled bloke got ripped up small and dropped on the fire when nobody was looking. Hell, I was crippled myself, wasn't I?

And I went around the same as before as though nothing had happened, nursing the little secret, the female contact I couldn't possibly tell anybody about. The seed of hope. Breathing on it, magnifying it, working on it already in a thousand ways, this wonderful and vital illusion we need so much. The second letter when it came made me smile like a child—I could actually feel it happening, the germination. The illusion had taken root, it was real, more real than reality. How happy she was to get my letter: she'd read it twice, three times, unable to believe how very lucky she was. Please write again, but only if you feel you want to in your heart. ' In your heart '—what a thing to say. She ended by saying that it would be dreadful stopping now or being disappointed when her heart *sang with hope* —she really did use those phrases—but perhaps it would be better to go no further, less cruel . . . Did I mean what I said? Was I sure, could it be true I genuinely needed her letters? That's what she was yearning to know. Oh yes, and would I tell her more about myself, my likes and dislikes. Her favourite book was *Sorrel and Son*. A p.s.— dare she ask me for a photograph of myself? I didn't dare read her letters twice as she did mine, I read them once, very fast, then shoved them away out of sight quick, so that her ghastly old-maidish way of putting things didn't interfere with the sincerity, heartbreaking, and so that my imagination could get to work. The correspondence with Edwina blossomed as rapidly as the one with the art student wilted. Almost overnight I mastered the art of reassurance. The event I dreaded, yet waited for daily, was the arrival of her own photo, promised in exchange for mine. Love, we ended each time, and much later it was Your Loving . . . Still no photo. Then, ever so gently one time she reproached me for not calling her Dearest. Coy as a maiden aunt she promised her photo as a reward : I was being bribed. So I gave her full measure, My Dearest One, and the wishing and wanting had gone so far I didn't care any more. Christ, I half meant it, I'm sure I did. More than half. Who else was there apart from her, who did I have to confess to, open my heart to? You are the one, my daft drippy one, you know me now, my dearest one, I am at your mercy, in your care. Oh it was easy, nice and easy. When I wrote it there was nothing wrong, it flowed off my pen truly, for that instant, the stroke of the heart coincided with the stroke of the pen. I was close to tears. Writing My Dearest One affected me so much that the letter I wrote under it was the most loving she ever had from me. Her letter came speeding back in the next post, straight as an arrow of desire.

I opened the envelope in the secrecy of the lav, but sat on the seat first because of the gravity, the solemnity of the occasion. Grabbed it tremblingly and stared at it with my whole face—a bit of blurred card, a snapshot of her in a deckchair on some grass, under an arch of trellis plaited with rose briars, it looked like. Roses! And the floppy white hat she wore, her face out of focus, pale, shrinking back into the shadow of the brim—how gentle and modest it was, how quaint, and so typical. Like a letter from her, exactly. My eyes bored ruthlessly at it—to hell with illusions—trying to ferret out the truth. No good, I could stare at it all day and I'd never really see anything. This pathetic little snap told me one thing though, something I'd known right away and refused to admit. Her gentility. She was genteel and nice and romantic, in an absolutely inoffensive, pitiful way. Here was the proof of it, staring at me. So what? She loved me, didn't she? And I remembered her letter, forgotten in the excitement, took it out and read it and yes oh yes she loves me, more than ever now because she's got my photo, it's in her handbag and it goes everywhere she goes, and she's glad, she's terribly happy, the birds are singing and am I happy now that I have her photo too? Am I glad? It went on and on, clean daft, nine pages of it. And I was under the spell of it, for the first time, genuinely moved by *her* words, not mine.

Very carefully I stuffed the letter back into the envelope. Gently slipped in the blurry snap. Got up and yanked the chain, because after all I'd been in there for a hell of a time, and shuffled out, taking care not to look in the mirror because if I saw my face I should see the truth and I'd want to howl. Downstairs my mother breaking her heart quietly over me for having secrets, punishing me with silence. And it would get worse, not better. I was dying by inches, I had to get out : home was a prison, every comfort to keep you warm and safe and happy and all you want to do is break out. But I was shit-scared already of what I'd tasted of the outside—six years of factory life, a fair slice, the whole country littered with prisons like that, from one end to the other. Wander through the town on a weekday and it was uncanny how doglike you felt, how lost without a leash and collar, wandering along the pavements through the crowd of women and old men, schoolboys zigzagging up and down and the feeling of rush and purpose, everybody belonging to a prison of some kind, either just leaving it or running back there again. To be on your own in the middle of that lot was like roaming around in space, cut off from human kind, shut out of a closed community. The loneliness was terrible, the tide of traffic pulsing and flooding, a grey flood of faces rushing for hearth and home every night, lovers wrapped around each other—where could you take your love before it curdled, who wanted it? The world is a prison, the men with ashes tipped over their ugly cropped heads stand in long rows, speechless, not even grunting, drowning there without a word in din and stink, minding the machines that drill and stamp and hammer and cut into their days, and their eyes are cold snake eyes, their cheeks venomous, the hide of their necks loose and scored and pock-marked with dead boils, and their mouths drag down at the corners, the vinegary bastards. The nightmare

68

is to end up like them—but outside you wander through space, on and on, utterly lost and separate, and come crawling back begging for the leash and collar.

The blurred face in the distance which simply asks for love, your love, is precious after all. Keep it out of sight, hide the truth, don't falter, don't ask questions—aren't you lonely enough yet? And the letters are posted and delivered, and you know the day is drawing nearer when you'll have to get on a train and go there, meet, and the thought fills you with dread. But nothing is worse than nothing. Make something happen—it might be worse than before or it might be better: who cares? Just something happening to prove to yourself that it's not too late. I'm still one of the living, me, half dead at twenty-one. I can function; try me. I can suffer as well as the next man, I can laugh and cry, bleed, drink tea. It's the nothingness that terrifies. The terror of being stranded on the bank in the prime of life, helpless to move a muscle, watching the blood gush freely. Waiting, waiting for a call. The thought gnawing that maybe you are deficient in some vital part, like a brand-new machine that's been tested and found dud. Standing at the bench with your head bowed over a tricky job, worrying at it, you pray between your teeth: Push me in, I can't stand this much longer. Christ, what's wrong with me? I want to swim with the others!

Ashes and rubies. It's like that at twenty-one. Ashes in the mouth, cold rain, fist banging on the stone, unable to speak, find words, choking with it one minute, the black night like a hole, life full of holes, smashed light bulbs, rotten teeth, red rust, and the next minute glowing all over like a ruby and laughing like a saint, in love with the loony jigsaw.

I sat in the train jogging over the points on the outskirts, in a muck sweat. Could have been in one of Hitler's cattle-trucks rolling towards the ovens, the way I felt. Why? What was the matter with me? I was licking my lips feverishly, sick with tension, heart thudding like a drum. For the fourth or fifth time I wiped the sweat off my palms. Would I recognise her on the platform? Bound to—it was only a one-eyed place, not much more than a halt. Condemned, I looked out bleakly at the grime and dirt, ripped ground, then raw new roads and blank concrete, new council houses, wire and concrete fences, compounds for the knobbly sprouts and grimy cabbages to stand to attention in, ragged flapping stumps. Here it comes, yards and sidings, a pile of cable drums, a junk heap like a tank where they emptied scrap iron, bashed-in car bodies, dead boilers, stove pipes, gas cookers. Rolling into the station, and it slid up to meet us, deathly quiet and inexorable.

No sign of her anywhere. I got off the train. Suddenly she was there beside me—where had she come from, out of the clouds?—fluttering, agitated, breathless, flushed. So close, her face only a few inches from me, that at first the shock didn't register. She was old! Much older than me—I was no good at guessing ages and it may have been her round-shouldered figure—she was shrunken, bent, musty, her bones looked frail and brittle. The soft, thin hair clung to her cheeks, she seemed to be hiding in it like a little old lady. I walked along with her, stunned. I went slowly, because she walked with difficult, hobbling steps like an invalid. The nightmarish quality of it all stopped me from speaking; I just gulped and struggled with my face, letting her chatter in a babyish breathless voice, calling me by my first name as if she owned me, was on intimate terms—this crone! I wanted to turn round and jump on the train and shout through the window : I'll be back, I'm sorry, there's been a terrible mistake. I could still feel the handshake, the tiny bundle of rheumatic bones she offered me, coyly cringing and squeaking and smiling ' Hello, Colin—you've come ! You're right on time !'

A little speech of welcome came gushing out of her mouth as we went those few yards to the ticket collector. She used it up in a matter of seconds, and then there was nothing, absolutely nothing. The thing was killed stone dead before we even got off the platform. I suppose she could see the whole story on my face, unless she was half blind like me. We went through the barrier and into the street and then, from then on, it was the funeral march up to her place, a pre-war council estate, the straight rows bisecting each other at regular intervals, and dead flat and tight and orderly, so that you longed to see something with a twist in it. Square little faded brick homes with wooden bays, or flat-fronted, every one from the same mould, same wire fences of square mesh. As soon as the station disappeared from sight I was lost, no bearings. It was Saturday afternoon and I saw one old bloke with crutches and a dog on a lead crossing the road ahead of us, and that's all. We were going past a pillar box on the flat damp pavement in this waste of silence when Edwina blurted out :

' That's where I put my letters !'

It was a gruesome last attempt to resurrect the romance. I followed the direction of her pointing finger as if that was the only way I could see it, nodded as I stared dumbly at the sleek red sides, the square-cut corners of its Fo-dog mouth, loathing its greedy fat belly for aiding and abetting. I kept staring, not having the guts to look at her. The forced note of gaiety cut into me like a shriek. I went limp with relief when she stopped at her gate. A bungalow.

Her mother, a big, blunt-spoken woman, came out of the kitchen and shook hands with me, then went blundering round in the tiny living-room of this doll's house re-arranging things, as nervous as her daughter but putting a defensive attack into her movements. She would rest her beefy fists on her hips and ask a question suddenly, brutally direct. Edwina scurried about, twittery and grotesque, patting her hair and running for the family album—blotted out completely by her mother. I saw in a flash what it was, how she'd lived in the shadow of this woman ever since her father had died, ever since her sister had left home to go nursing, ever since her brother had pushed off abroad—there he was with his colleagues, in his white shirt and shorts, swart frowning face like his mother, framed and deathless on top of the piano. India. A missionary, he was. Somebody smoothed and patted the settee and I sat there, family history was poured at me, the females hard at it, Edwina almost relaxed now on her own ground. There were even some spiteful-sounding rejoinders now and then, masked by her cracked spinsterish laugh, a running battle that continued between the two of them, I imagined—though I didn't have any clues so it was lost on me—and it couldn't be stopped now, with a gentleman caller in the house, any more than they could stop the tap dripping. Edwina would glance at me after one of these spiteful jabs, and she'd duck her head and blush apologetically, smiling her ghostly photograph-smile. It made me shudder, but apart from those moments I was struggling to live with the horror of the situation, make the best of it—it was bearable with her mother there between us.

Somehow the farce came to an end—the longest, most painful week-end I ever spent. Saturday night we went back through the ruled streets to a cinema, queued for three-quarters of an hour in grim silence, sat through it side by side in the dark like two liners that pass in the night, never touching, ablaze with trapped life, engines thumping madly. Letting ourselves back into the place again we found the light on in the living-room, sandwiches under a plate on the table and, planted bang in the middle like a vase, a bottle of stout specially for me. For me—the man of the house! And on the sideboard the current issue of the church magazine.

I stuck it out till Sunday afternoon, the time I was supposed to leave anyway—couldn't think of an excuse for leaving earlier. Long before that, though, it had sunk in: she didn't come to say good-bye at the station. And she didn't get another word from me. The ground swallowed me up. Cruel, despicable—but it didn't matter by then what a bastard I was, my one desire was to get rid of her. No more lies on paper—my lies had caught and choked me, I'd paid. I took it all back home, the self-disgust, the shame, like an unspeakable bag of dirty washing I wasn't going to let anybody see, ever. If I'd pretended, put on an act and then slowly, bit by bit, from a distance . . . but my stomach wouldn't take it. Anyway, I was sure she knew. That last glance of reproach or resignation or whatever it was, before she ducked back inside and closed the door— I can still see it. It disintegrated me. No, it needn't have happened but it did and it wasn't her fault, it wasn't mine either, or anybody's—just life playing a dirty trick on us both. The worst part of the lot was the silence and the mute acceptance, not being insulted, accused, spat at, having to imagine it and then do it yourself, a thousand times.

I bet they pushed her about at work, made a drudge of her. 'Edwina, come on, *move*!' How did she cope with things like phone calls? 'Edwina, always ask who it is at the other end.' 'I did, I did.' 'Well, who was it?' 'I couldn't hear what they said.' 'That's because you listen too hard—and you're a bag of nerves to begin with.' And she'd hang her head, go back to her corner and sit quietly. I could imagine it. I bet that big healthy sod of a brother kicked her around when he lived at home. I bet she let him. Even her catty little jabs at her mother aren't really meant to hurt, they're spoken innocently; no claws out, no idea of the score. Her mother could send her flying with one swipe, anyway. And if she did, I bet Edwina would scramble up and say *she* was sorry, her soft brown eyes bright with forgiveness.

She looked wizened, old, antiquated, older than her mother sometimes, but it was her childishness that made me aware quite soon that she was cracked. This defenceless child in her struck terror into me and it shamed me: every action of mine seemed brutal and calculated. I don't mean she was right round the twist—not like a navvy I used to see when I was a kid, bouncing down our street with springy animal strides, great floury boots and short legs in a trance, his cap set dead level and under it those huge watery eyes of his, bright with amazement or terror, I could never decide. The Mole, they called him. On site he worked nonstop all day, so I heard, sweat pouring off him; would go through his dinner-break if his mates let him. At knocking-off time they had to stop him again and hang his knapsack round his neck and push him through the stockade gate into the road and he was all right if he faced in the right direction, off he went home, his tragic Van Gogh boots slamming up and down, cap screwed tight on his grey cropped head which he held well lowered, arms and shoulders working, working. Human Mole. Donkey. Carthorse. Mule. I saw him break into a gallop once, leaping over the uncharted macadam from one pavement to the other like a hunted kangaroo.

There was a girl during the war—a Lillington girl—and

I had just the same impulse then, to get right away. I suppose that's the reaction of any healthy organism. I didn't know she was off her nut at first, and she was, this one: I mean completely. I saw her several times on the bus—she'd get off at Kenilworth—and thought she looked a bit odd, that's all. England's crammed full of odd-looking people. Pale puffy face, nut-crackery. How old was she? It was that part again which was wrong, the age thing. Then once when the bus happened to be jammed tight she was standing up near me hanging on to the strap, swaying slightly more than normal. I may have started watching her more closely all of a sudden for this reason. Soon my nerves tingled, I was riveted on her. She hadn't done anything but now I knew something was wrong. There was an awful tension, something terribly cock-eyed was happening right under my nose. She twisted her head this way and that. It was hot and close, a rattletrap of a bus, men smoking, not a window open.

'I've got to get out,' she said suddenly, calmly and loudly.

It was a public announcement, peremptory. I shivered, it struck me as so grisly, and I found myself longing for her stop to come.

'I can't breathe,' came a second announcement, louder.

My teeth were grinding together. Any minute now she'll throw a fit or dive headlong through the glass, I thought. Everybody deliberately not hearing, not looking, in that sickening manner we have, either from decency or hypocrisy—you can never tell with an Englishman. That isn't surprising, because they don't know themselves, and they don't want to know. And if the truth were known it's probably a bit of each. They'd rather die than acknowledge a sneaky fart to be theirs, partly out of shame and partly because they can't bear to embarrass the other fellow. Better ignore it completely—pretend it never happened, like Nelson. Like him they were all equipped, man, woman and child, with a blind eye. I was the same only different; I was looking, only with me it was sheer fright. Bunched up tight as a watch spring, ready for anything. Nothing happened, she got off at the right place, stepped down like a normal person and walked off, and I relaxed, shakily off the hook.

Another time she seemed to be in conversation with a couple of older girls who knew her. More people got on, the three girls were pushed up the gangway nearer to me. I got a ringside seat. They were baiting her with a few questions for a giggle. One was saying, ' I like fruit gums, Hazel, don't you?'

' Yes, I like fruit gums. I like pastilles too. I like cashews as well. Cashews remind me of birdseed.'

Giggles and big-eyed glances. ' They do?'

' I mean ants' eggs.'

' Really?'

' I don't know what you mean.'

' Anyway you like them.'

' What?'

' Cashews—you just said so.'

' Well I can't remember things. I can't remember, can't remember.'

Then a lull, so they had another prod and a stir. You little lousebound bastards, I said to myself, sitting there against them with my listening ear not far off the belly-button of this smart piece. They were off again :

' Do you like birdseed then, Hazel?'

' Oh no, horrible. I don't like dog food either.'

Wonderful, but there was better to come, and without any prompting. The public announcement voice again :

' There's a peculiar smell in here.'

Shrieks of mirth over my head, the two bright little bitches half collapsing on each other.

' Is there? Perhaps it's your feet.'

Shocked at this, she cried out in what I guessed must have been a pure echo of her mother :

' You mustn't say things like that!'

' Why not?'

' It's rude.'

There came a spell of chatter which would have seemed perfectly normal to a casual listener. I wasn't casually listening though, I was half straining my tabhole off. ' I'm going to do Christmas shopping today,' she said, and that was fine, nobody could swop sly looks. But she had to go and tag on, 'to get Christmas stuff.' Towards the end of the trip she came out with really preposterous things, like 'Why is it raining?' and 'We should stay indoors when it's bad weather like this. Why don't we?'

I was always glad when she got out, she scared me, caught on my nerves, and though I couldn't care less what she came out with, personally, the world of others who did, sitting all around in judgement, made it a big strain; so I didn't like it. I wanted her to shut up. The word for this feeling is embarrassment. Yes, I was glad to see the back of her. Then afterwards like a hypocrite I was sorry for her and thought how much better she was than those sly cagey bitches who kept doubling up with attacks of the giggles. They were only passing the time, it's true, and I suppose she was oblivious anyway. I was a fool, getting worked up for nothing. Merry Christmas! Happy New Year! She was at least sixteen, black-haired, dressed like a little girl, pallid straight legs in ankle socks, bull-nosed shoes, a kid's woollen bonnet on her head. Clambering down from the bus she was terribly stiff-legged and cautious, no suppleness at all: more like an old girl of eighty.

13

AFTER Edwina I made sure of the body first. I wasn't exactly callous—I mean I didn't go deliberately shopping for it or anything like that. I was a hard innocent. I saw this girl Kay, playing tennis with her pal, another teenager. Kay, the pouter pigeon. She had a peaches-and-cream complexion, she bulged fore and aft and she was only nineteen, still growing. Could have been puppy fat but it was still real, her plump titties bounced up and down inside her cream blouse in a generous, jolly sort of motion. I studied them more than the ball as she charged around red in the face, whooping, socking the ball back ineffectually. Her partner was short, and much more purposeful. I wasn't struck on her.

Like all my forced friendships it was abortive, doomed

to frustration, this one. I joined the tennis club so that I didn't have to keep staring through the mesh. The biggest obstacle was her friend, who stuck like glue—they were both training to be librarians. When I got a date with Kay we had to take Valerie with us the first evening. I suppose Kay must have had a little chat with her between then and the next occasion, because when I asked where Valerie was, out came an unlikely story about a sick aunt she'd had to rush off and see all of a sudden.

Kay was bespoke, she was a frozen virgin, her father had died earlier that year and her mother was in bed suffering from shock. Things were under a cloud, to say the least. Kay was sexless with tragedy, devotion, self-sacrifice, and various morbid thoughts and preoccupations concerning death. Her breasts bounced in a jolly way and no mistake, but independently of her, with a perverse life of their own. She was a kind of mirage. We went for gloomy walks across the fields behind Orley. Once she had to clip the grass on her father's new grave, so I trailed with her up the freshly raked and weeded gravel paths one Saturday afternoon, in a cool breeze. Then we got on our bikes and cycled over to the bloody fields again, for more silent walking. You idiot, I kept telling myself. That afternoon I bought her a peach and she ate it soundlessly, curled in the grass, without spilling a drop. Her large moony eyes with their vaguely reproachful expression avoided me, and the only time she ever spoke warmly was when she got on to the subject of Chris, a fellow student at the librarians' training college.

'I can't stop thinking about him,' she told me. 'What do *you* think I ought to do? Should I tell him how I feel about him or not? He probably isn't even aware of my existence. What would you do in my place?'

She took me in to see her mother once, while I was hanging around waiting for her to get herself ready. She led me into the boxy bedroom on the ground floor at the front of the house and left me to make conversation as best as I could. There was her mother, yellowish, black marks under her eyes, propped up on the pillows and smiling weakly. The resemblance to her daughter was amazing—even to the reproach in her eyes. It was life they were accusing mutely, both of them, in a fundamental complaint they had no words for. How cruel and heartless, their eyes said. I stood there at the foot of the bed, racking my brains for something to say. I took off my cycle clips as a sign of respect.

'Hello, young man,' she said. 'What a lovely day!'

If it wasn't her mother, or her father's grave, it would be this Chris—I loathed him already—she was mooning over. I didn't touch her once—not even a goodnight kiss. If she wanted to freeze me out, I kept saying to myself, then why does she let me go trailing round with her like this? It was unreal. All that flesh, and you had the feeling that if you poked a finger at her you'd go right through. Nothing there. Absent. In any case she was untouchable. I'd no more have wanted to slip my hand up her dress than fart at Sunday School; it was just unthinkable. Long before I admitted it to myself, my tool realised what a fiasco it all was. Even lying in bed thinking about her I never once got an erection; not even first thing in the morning.

I was ripe for the pros. Yet with years of instruction in the factory, the street, hanging around at street corners, I was still a novice in the art of being tough. Still a skinned rabbit. Two features, eyes and lips, betrayed me every time I came face to face with a 'situation'. I couldn't stare people in the face like my pals did without flinching, I had no hard fixed gaze to dish out, I couldn't flick those razor-sharp glances, or tell somebody flatly to 'fuck off'. Yet I was getting more like them, the cyanide was case-hardening me, it was only a matter of time. In the dinner hour there was a small gang of us apprentices, four or five. We'd queue up for the canteen dinner—you went to one tin counter and bought tickets first, main meal, pudding, tea— and sit together at the long unpainted trestles, then get to work. Abusing it, naturally, that was the thing :

'Where's the bleedin' meat then?'

'There it is, you cunt, under them carrots.'

'Christ I thought it was a shadow.'

You spread your elbows, kept your head down over the plate like a dog sticking its snout in the dish, and chewing away it didn't matter if your mouth was open or shut, or how much noise you made. Afterwards it was the grunt, sigh, plate shoved away as if with contempt, and a ripe belch or two if you felt like it :

' Ah, that's better—excuse a pig.'

There was a feeling of rancour. If you spoke to your mates it had to be jeering, violent. Insults were spat out freely, as a matter of course, in a joyless kind of humour, and you retaliated in the same way, loud-mouthed, hard, or kept quiet. There was no freedom, nobody relaxed or spoke in confidence; none of that stuff to do with homes and girls, mothers, the female. The bitter taste was on our tongues, the iron hook dug in cruelly. We were men, in a man's world, but with one terrible disadvantage: we were virgins. Not knowing how to cope we kept spitting words, aiming blows, lashing out at friends if they came too close or noticed too much, saw what a green kid you were :

' Fuck off, you cunt.'

It was a howling travesty of how we really were inside, under the masks, and there was no breaking the rigid pattern of behaviour laid down for us, as clear and fixed as the white lines of the gangways.

My eyes were no good, a soft brown, soft and yielding, but much worse were my lips. The lips of my mouth. I had no more control over them than a man with no teeth. At times of stress my mouth just collapsed, the lips wobbled like a baby's, horribly out of control. Again and again it disgraced me. I choked with eloquence, burned with desperate locked fire, I was tender as a lamb, stiff with young pride; I'd show a woman, she'd be wild with gratitude when she unlocked me—my hands glowed with the knowledge of what I was, hands of power. And there was this lady's mouth caving in, pouting, drooping piteously at the corners as if it was going to cry.

After the grub, we'd either play pontoon or go for a stroll and a breath of air in the side streets. Walk out past the closed serving hatches with our backs to the stage. If there was a soprano screeching for dear life up there then Lou would probably give her the V-sign, keeping his fingers close to his head as a precaution, in case she twisted round at the crucial moment in his direction. Then he'd be giving his scalp a scratch, his face deadpan. He was our comic. I'd be a mixture of pity and hatred for these third-rate performers who were supposed to be keeping up our morale and helping the war effort. Didn't they have a clue about working men, what they were like? Why couldn't somebody tell them the score? We slouched along, legs too far apart like young colts, down the canteen steps and out : then it was either the back way, trailing through the factory outbuildings, or straight on to the highway, the big trunk connection with the outside. We went out raggedly, no direction in particular, as if our feet were taking us for a walk. We were killing time. It was unreal, being let out at this time of day. Nothing had released us, we were merely out for exercise. On the trunk, but not travelling, not using it to go anywhere. Hands stuck in our pockets, we swaggered, dragged our feet, kicked a fag packet along with us, dribbling, passing—all with a studied lack of interest. We cultivated the air of louts; this was the act fixed for us, a ritual of long standing, till we reached manhood and got married, loaded with responsibilities. This was the uneasy interim. If anything female and young enough tripped by, the instinct was to degrade it, drag it down :

' Jesus, she's pale—I bet she's got the jam rags on.'

If it looked rough, a vicious chorus of insults rose up.

' I bet her fanny's like a horse's collar.'

' She's rough enough for any dog to tackle.'

' If you fucked her, bugger me—it'd be like stirring a bucket of whitewash.'

The best at it was Ray, who shaved morning and night and had a real man's jowl, already bristly and black by dinnertime. He had an endless stream of foul remarks, uttered calmly, harsh and firm and intractable. His gait was angry, caged, explosive. He tried to dawdle like the rest of us, but after a bit he'd burst out in a seizure of rage at the one lagging behind :

' Come on, man, for fuck's sake !'

He gave the most brutal impression of a man without any forcing, he was all ready to enter the world, yet like us he hadn't been anywhere or done anything, except get drunk. There was that chin of his, rough as emery cloth.

Yet he wasn't a thug: far from it. His clouded, defensive eyes were gentle, with long curly lashes, and now and then he stuttered. You sensed that his violence was directed inwards.

We went haunting the streets, shackled invisibly, drifting round corners like shadows, and in the winter especially we stayed away from the main arteries where the traffic rammed through indifferent to us, long-distance heavies, big stuff. These were rancid, poor days. We hated the vacuity but it caught us, and our arrogance took on an edge like an east wind. Outside we really felt poverty-stricken, directionless, we watched the free purposeful lorries and it made us worse. The contrast dehumanised us. Inside the beehive it was work, din, stink, chat, real solitude, the cup of tea and the fag, a sly visit to a mate on another section right out of sight, trips to the shithouses—and you had a good selection. It was better inside, living and breathing, human; it was where you belonged. Nobody was free, nobody could get out. It was equal and all right.

Nine years. Imagine thirty, forty years in a single span. Who'd stick a sentence like that in their right mind if they knew it was definite, a fact? Nobody knows how long they've actually got. It's day to day. Add it up later, reckon the score, and you try to feel shocked but don't really, because it's history now. Used up. Tomorrow's knocking on the door—hang on, I'm coming. Answer the door, quick, you might have won the pools. Millions to one but it could be you; somebody wins it every week. It could be you. Nobody admits they're under sentence. Who could bear it?

Nine years. Gone in one snap, gobbled up by Mr Purlham, white-haired, stiff-backed, rosy-cheeked self-made industrialist, with his pop-eyed glare of a fanatic, his canteen speeches and his sleek nephew at his right hand. The crazy empire-builder, Adam's apple gulping in his stringy old throat like a danger signal. Choking on his own will power, drive, ambition. Towards the end his nephew, fresh from the army, starts appearing by his side on the canteen platform. Blond, plump and glossy like an otter, with none of the fiery monomania of the old man, who makes an effort to control himself and speak calmly but still storms

F

at the eyeballs, still stiffens his old neck at the sound of jeers from the back; tyrannical as ever, forcing the men into sullen silence and obedience by his old master's trick of just standing there in a smoulder of disgust, refusing to speak. Then the withering contempt as he opened, and you knew what came after, the trampling and bending and dismissing of the hostility in a pep talk that opened and closed with a threat:

'Don't think I can't deal with people who are too rowdy to let me speak . . .'

A whole world, remember—even its own barber. This was to cut down on absenteeism during the war, when the six-day weeks were being worked by everybody, and a man would have to take a day off to get his hair cut. Own barber, own surgery, canteen, social club, police, fire brigade, big and small outbuildings and still growing, sheds, stores, boiler houses, pill-boxes, shelters, dug-outs, all with roads between. A complex. The dispatch and packing came first, as you entered through the main doors over the wood-block floor soaked in machine oil, studded with lathe cuttings, milling chips, capstan swarf, drill curls, iron filings, steel, brass, copper, aluminium. Gangways marked out in white lines, fading here and there, freshened up for Royal visits. Punch clocks and racks of clock cards and notice boards carrying warnings, dotted about strategically. The Ordnance Department, Aviation Department, Dispatch, Millwrights, Horizontal Millers, Vertical Millers, Borers, Turning Shop. Paint Shop, Test Bay, Inspectors, Press Tools, Injection, Teleprinters, Machine Tool, Progress Chasers, Time and Motion, Surface Grinders, Internal Grinders, External Grinders, Screwcutters. Capstan Section, Shapers, Fitters, Precision Tool, Hardening Shop, Sandblasting, Apprentice School, Experimental, Auto, Design Department, Projection, Stores. Vertical Planers, Horizontal Planers, Radial, Broach, Testers.

And shithouses. Dotted about strategically like the boards and punch clocks, but every one built against an outer wall. Some with urinals, the porcelain trough clogged with fag ends, matches, fag packets, the water squirting and farting out of the brass sprinklers to dilute the rivers of piss, swilling round the garbage and draining off somehow. Some with no urinal but a filthy encrusted wash basin. Some without either wash basin or urinal—just a row of bogs like horse boxes. Each shithouse reeking of poison gas first thing, with all the booths occupied and going full blast, but otherwise each one different from the next, with a character of its own. It's funny but I can't recall now what we used for paper in those places, whether a roll supplied by the firm, bearing their name, or newspaper, or what. They didn't give anything away, that firm, and if toilet rolls had been provided they'd have been lifted the same day for certain, name or no name. In the shithouses nearest to the main gates there were no doors on the booths, and for a long time I wondered if they'd been pinched, or unscrewed by the management so as to make our stay as short as possible. Then one morning I looked closer at the door jamb, there were no screw holes, so it looked as if the bastards had put the things up without doors to begin with. For a bit of privacy you sat on the throne with the morning paper spread out in front of you. Wandering down the line of pans looking for a vacancy first thing that's all you'd see : rows of newspapers, boots, fingers, dangling braces, concertina trousers. So there was no lingering, no chance for graphic art either on the walls or door. But they made up for it in the others. Every inch of space seemed to be decorated, some of it with crabbed, tiny scrawl, sloping down steeper and steeper, till you were nearly standing on your head to read it, and sometimes the whole back of a door occupied by a lavish sketch of a pair of tits. Swelling, rampant images were attempted, and when the artist couldn't get the proportions right or the realism convincing he got desperate and drew on a bigger scale. Pricks hung their bloated heads and dripped spunk in thick gobbets; cunts yawned, as if on the point of giving birth, and one or two were carnivorous, equipped with a set of teeth by wits. ' It makes you think with all this wit that Shakespeare has been here to shit.' One of the longest stories was on the brickwork where the downpipe from the cistern was fastened. It had been gouged out with a steel scriber, by the look of it, then the grooves inked in crudely with indelible

pencil. Maybe several hands had a go at it. Because it had
to find space where it could it wound down in a spiral to
the left of the pan, then petered out; a characteristic fantasy about a man who puts up for the night at his brother's
flat. 'One night I got stranded in the town where my
brother lived so I called and asked if he would put me up
for the night he said yes I could sleep in his bed with him
if I liked and his wife would sleep on the living-room sofa
which is what I did Well next morning he left early to go
to work and I was flaked out asleep dead tired when suddenly I felt a hand on my thigh creeping round softly so I
did nothing anyway I was too drowsy then I felt the same
hand taking a handful of my balls then my cock which was
soft as shit I just lay there lovely and warm wondering what
the game was not that I cared would you And suddenly
she was rubbing her tits up and down on my back then her
leg wrapped round me I knew then who it was my
brother's wife the randy little bitch Oh Tom she moaned
I'm dying for it can't you get a hard-on and she no sooner
said that than I started to I was stiff as a ramrod in no
time where the strength came from I'll never know She was
delighted I kept telling her it was no good I was too tired
to fuck her oh never mind she said I'll fuck you and she
did what a hot bitch she was . . .'

Well, it was here my good father delivered me in all
innocence, on January 1st, at the tender age of fifteen. Innocent as babes, both of us. He had gone through it with
the rest, that legendary Slump everybody in our family referred to—it was one long slump between the wars as far as
I could make out—and though living in Brum and the El
Dorado had saved him to some extent, the experience was
branded on him like an injury, an attribute. He'd sunk low
enough at one point to tramp the streets doing door-to-door
canvassing for the *Express*. He was never out, even in the
worst times, more than a few months. That was not long
after they were married, and it broke up the marriage for
a while; they had to separate and go back to living with
their parents while he tried his luck in another town. Anyway it was bitter, it marked them, now it was over and
done with, and when they brought it out it was to adorn

themselves with it as an attribute, and put the fear of God into the kids. The factory was bound to be the place to take me. Live, humming, desirable—it would drag him there by instinct, it was deeply in him from his young struggling days as a family man, along with Labour and the Slump and the war to end wars. The idea was stuck in his head that I ought to have a trade : he was for ever telling my mother in front of me that if he'd had one he'd have been kicked around a lot less. I was passive and victim-like, I waited in the concrete pill-box just inside the gates, sniffing with vague dread like an animal smelling the blood. They were fetching the Apprentice Supervisor. In he bustled, not a minute to lose, his white butcher's smock stained at the pockets with industry, the grime of iron in his fingernails. He frowned, then smiled just with the edges of his lips, leaving his eyes dead. Saying something he showed his tobacco-stained, spaced-out fangs, and that was a slight improvement. He stuck out a long skinny hand for my father to shake. I stared at his knobbly wrist thick with black hairs, until his horse jaw, working about sideways in a laborious chewing motion, started to fascinate me. Lugubrious Bristolian speech was being manufactured, leaden with phoney gravity. His eyes glinted grimly, flicking over me, the new brat. ' Quite frankly, your son will receive the best engineering training it's possible to have in this town. I can assure you of that. If he's keen and industrious, you understand, I can be perfectly honest and say that you won't have cause to regret bringing him to us. I can assure you on that point.' Turning to me :

' Are you keen, son?'

' Yessir.'

' Not afraid of work?'

' No, sir.'

It was settled. He rubbed his dry hands together like a workhouse master, then started washing them with invisible soap to keep the circulation going—it was cold where we stood, we were bundled in overcoats and I could see him shivering. He hung there, slack at the knees, his chest caved in, the top pocket of his white coat bristling with rules, pencils, gauges. He was all of a twitch because he was freezing, but also because he couldn't bear to be idle. Skin and grief. Another twitch, fangs again, and he was gone.

When I really got to know him though he wasn't all that bad. Funereal was the word for him. The other lads referred to him as Father to convey the episcopal voice and his habit of winding his fingers together and holding his hands while he walked. What I liked best about him was his preoccupation: he was too absorbed in problems to bother much with mere apprentices—he left that to his chargehands. He had a glassed-in box and he sat in there hatching schemes, having little secret conferences with his staff or sitting hunched over his desk in solitary state holding his head in his hands. Seeing him like that we used to say, 'Father's crying again' because it was exactly the attitude. It was easy to keep out of his way; you soon learned how to merge, be inconspicuous.

We were in a compound called the School, a corner of one of the main sheds, and it was charming if you could see it that way, like a model village, perfectly scaled, but with the reality of a real village sucked out of it. On the other side of the fence—and we could see it through the mesh, hear it and smell it, even if we couldn't touch it— was the throbbing world of men. Massive broaching machines out there groaned and shrieked, with queer lulls in between, and then blokes could be heard calling across to each other, letting out jeers, catcalls, guffaws, and if a chorus of wolf whistles rose up you could bet it was a woman going down the main aisle, haughty and statuesque or loose and jaunty or doing the rhumba, red-cheeked or indifferent or yelling back a mouthful, according to how seasoned she was. Our nursemaids the chargehands, who belonged out there and were only wet-nursing us because it was a soft number and paid a bit better, would exchange knowing looks and gaze through the mesh at the haze of blue smoke over the big howling machines as if yearningly. It was like being in a monastery for them. Swearing was against the rules, so were dirty stories; they swore and swapped filth just the same, but on the sly, and you could see how they resented that. They'd straddle their legs and have a quick smoke—that wasn't encouraged either—with their eyes sliding restlessly over their toy domain. Everything was in miniature in that place. We had our own stores, a boy storekeeper in charge. If he wouldn't cough up with more than one sheet of emery cloth there'd be scuffles over the low fence with somebody keeping an eye on the glass booth. The chargehands obligingly looked the other way. Unless it was serious, they were glad of any distraction. They had a secret language of derisive smiles which they exchanged across the compound, and they twitched their noses, raised eyebrows, worked in all kinds of refinements to express mockery and boredom. One, who had become a master of irony, used to shrug with marvellous eloquence as a sort of last word. How they loathed it, their little kingdom! The lathes, grinders, millers, shapers, bandsaw, benches were exactly the same as in the real factory, only smaller and cleaner altogether. Naturally there were no piece rates and no inspectors—we were playing at work.

There was a tall gawky youth they called Karl, a German refugee, whose English was stiff and formal like a public speech, and his black crinkly hair was cropped short and his neck was long, and stiff like his speech. He bent shortsightedly over his lathe, the most modern and gleaming, the biggest machine in the School, and the chargehands were deferential to him because his work was skilful and he was a favourite—his father had business connections with the firm. I didn't know any names or anything about the set-up, but in a day or two I could pick out the favourites by the way they stood and talked and strolled around. They had a proprietary air, like prefects at school, and they were haughty and so casual. These were the élite of our rarified little world. They lounged insolently against the best machines and spoke to the chargehands with their hands stuck in their pockets, as equals. When they went to the store and hung over the top of the barrier—they were all tall, naturally—the boy didn't argue the point as he did with the others. They got the best. The most intricate jobs were entrusted to them, jobs that would have made me tremble all over with fear and apprehension, terribly conscious of the precision, the fine tolerances, the critically

87

sharp lines of the blueprint *and its silence*, icily blue like a map of hell. I was beaten before I began. But not these boys. They twirled the handles and cut finely and surely, calm as surgeons. I admired them, and I marvelled at their cruel radiance. They were always the tallest and handsomest, we were runts in comparison, the rest of us. We loathed and worshipped, kept clear and would never have dreamed of approaching them, or marching up boldly to them, direct, to borrow a tool.

The boy who fascinated me at the very beginning in that model farmyard—a boy so useless at manual work that his father must have been dippy to put him to a trade—had a strange surname. I remember it as Xerri, and you pronounced it to sound like sherry. He was there three months and then disappeared : I think his parents left the district. Or it may have been that his old man came to his senses and found him a more suitable occupation. I didn't pal up with Don Xerri, it was only that I couldn't help watching him all the time. I gathered he was well off, compared to us. He had a boarding school voice, and his face, soft and pink and beautiful, was—I realise now—like the face of a very young Scott Fitzgerald. Perhaps it was because he seemed so incongruous dirtying the pale baby skin of his hands in a factory that I couldn't take my eyes off him. The languor of his gestures belonged to another world entirely : seeing him at work, or what he meant to pass for work, pretending to be industrious and trying to stifle his giggles, you saw that he'd never be any use if he stood there for ever. When he paused—which he did every other minute—and straightened his back there was such luxury in the movement that you couldn't help grinning your head off. Filing along a template, the simplest exercise for beginners, he held his file like a banana and still hadn't mastered this fundamental skill after three months. I was ignorant of the very word homosexual in those days, but to say he was one tells me no more now than it would have done then. There was something soft and very corruptible about him, and there was a glamorous sweetness. I imagined him nestling seductively against the breasts of his elegant mother, his smile glistening, his shapely head tousled, milky and soft and beautiful. He wasn't elegant himself, he was too small and approachable. Mostly he had this subtle and secretive smile, or he was giggling with some close pal like a lover. If he did burst out laughing, it was a soft explosion of sensuousness, opening his mouth and stretching his throat, showing his hard white teeth, abandoning his whole body to it.

One corner of the compound was glassed-in and had a ceiling, instead of sharing the roof trusses and dirty skylights of the main shop, and this room was actually a classroom, with rows of seats and a blackboard like a proper school. Once a week a teacher used to arrive, a plump dynamic little Russian, middle-aged, a bald dome pushing through his thinning locks, which were black and well-greased, and hung over his ears in wings like a musician's. He was a professor or doctor, anyway important, who ran a private school for girls. His passion was mathematics. He spoke about it so ardently that I used to actually look forward to him coming, his fire inspired me, and you could relax and listen and not make any headway, nobody bothered, there were no exams to worry about at the end of it. My maths didn't improve but for the first time I was on the point of tasting its raptures and appreciating its almost mystical satisfactions. At the heart of it was power, the power men feel in a clean orderly room with the sounds of life sealed off—ours was like that, muffled, faintly humming on the other side of the glass—and the white-ruled paper, the pen as sharp as a scalpel, cutting methodically at the problem, proving Euclid, setting out abstract perfections according to the gospels of Calculus, Differential, Integral, Infinitesimal. It was a universe of supreme order impervious to change and accident, fire and storm, pestilence, night sweat. Above life. The rigorous, passionate little foreigner taught us to ignore the world surging soundlessly at the windows. He was trying to raise us up, purify us, and it affected me like a religion. His other subject, practical engineering, was concerned with tools, cutting edges, varying angles of drill points for different materials. It was useful to us, had an obvious application, and for that reason his heart wasn't in it, you could tell. He lacked

89

fire, and I got bored and longed for the pure maths again, even though I knew I'd never master it.

Most of the week the lecture room was empty. Once I came back early from dinner and went in there to look for a pencil I'd lost. Over in a far corner, giggling softly, was Don Xerri with his chief pal, a bruiser with carroty hair and a red bull neck named Dawson, who was pushing him against the wall and mauling him, pawing at him with his ham fists. He turned his head and laughed, and I went out again quickly, confused, unable to look at Xerri's pale face, his sweet mouth and long-lashed eyes. I couldn't figure it out, what they were up to—that was how ignorant I was. Not long afterwards somebody passed on a pulp magazine for me to read—it was going the rounds like a chain letter, as these things did—and I slipped down the alleyway between the fences to the shithouse shared by apprentices and men. Locked in there, I read the stories by instalments during the day. It was a book for perverts—another world utterly foreign to me. Yet I read the incomprehensible details feeling hot and guilty, and my fingers shook as they turned the pages. Women in tiny frilled aprons that exposed their naked arses—' buttocks ' was a greatly favoured word, a key to the endless ritual—and other women with broad leather belts so tight they were gasping for breath, and others struggling to drag on boots as tight as gloves, so long they reached up to their crotches. Or they were being laced into corsets until their eyes bulged like Pekinese, while somebody joyfully beat those bared and offered buttocks. The theme was always the same : humiliation, flagellation, constriction. Pain and pleasure and punishment were inextricably mixed. Sickened and fascinated and lost, I passed it on, a dog-eared and ownerless manual. It burned in me for hours and then died of lack of fuel. My imagination couldn't function on no experience, so I suppose that saved me. While it lived I licked my lips and felt famished, I wanted more details, and at the same time the skin of my mind crawled in a kind of terror, as if I was contaminated with a disease.

The whole period was famished, pinched, hemmed around with fears and not knowing and the menace of beyond, where it was real and dirty and waiting. After six months or so you were automatically expelled and outposted to whichever section had a free machine or a spare bench, and later you might go back in the School again for another spell, but not for long. By accident I use the word spell and it's true that the word goes with that place; but the spell only worked the first time. Going back in again afterwards you were on a different level, you saw it with different eyes, through a fog of nostalgia, dispossessed, it was sadly irrelevant and midget and laughable and you walked carefully and gently like a Gulliver, your ears full of shrill cries. I never went back again to stay but I should have liked to, just to experience the Gulliver feeling.

I moved around, I was with turners one year, fitters the next. The richest time and the most unhealthy was on the machine grinders. I liked it because it was self-contained, and easy, nobody bothered you too much or stopped your daydreams, there was no machine oil flooding about, making your clothes stink and giving you the itch on the forearms and fingers. It was small enough to secrete yourself in, a section of say half a dozen blokes, including the chargehand, yet in the middle of the main shop indistinguishable from the rest with all its lanes, belts and motors, hundreds of men intent on their own tasks; then as the minute hand on those punch clocks crept up to six the furtive edging and drifting would begin—a secret coalescence. Two minutes to go and the boldest would walk up openly and plant themselves there, a *fait accompli*, tight against the racks of cards in a cheeky little queue. The most audacious would be the first one to make the move and arrive there, and as soon as he felt others begin to form up behind him—he didn't need to look—his hand would sneak up for his card from the rack. This would be a signal, the queue grew out faster behind his back, a long snake, while he watched that minute hand and waited tense as a sprinter for the gun. *Bang!* it jumped, the minute hand. His card moved that same instant and was in the slot and *bang!* he hit the punch lever, ripped out his card, found a home for it in the rack again, streaked off. *Bang! bang!* the clock was going. *Bang! bang!* and the stampede was away. That was the night, when old Purlham suddenly arose down the bottom end of the gangway, planted himself in the middle of the road to freedom, pop eyes blazing, his hand up like Canute as the flood bore down on him four abreast. 'Stop running!' he yelled. 'At once! I forbid it absolutely!' I wasn't there when it happened, I imagined it. Just the kind of thing the old fanatic would do. It nearly worked, too, but the faltering runners at the front couldn't put the brakes on quick enough, and even if they had their mates were in a trampling herd behind and they'd never have heard the old bastard, there was too much din, too many war cries, too much neighing of chargers, yells of delight, crazy hoots of laughter, girls whinnying and shrieking. He got knocked on one side and sat down with a thump. It was a wonder they didn't smash his arms or legs, trample all over him. I detested him, like the others, I wouldn't have shed a tear, but when they told me how he stood his ground, waving his arms and yelling like a lunatic, I had to admire his guts. Next day the warnings flowered on all the notice boards: instant dismissal for the next man caught running down the main gangways. So in future they walked, so fast it was the nearest thing to running I'd ever seen. They did it stiff-legged, clockwork fashion, legs working like mad scissors. After a week of that they were running naturally again, but not quite with the same joyous certitude: then it was only a matter of days till they were back to normal.

Outside, they funnelled through the gates and rushed in hunting packs for the buses, panting and victorious if they got themselves seats. If I was after a bus I didn't waste time either; it was a matter of keeping yourself upright in the torrent. But I was never first at the clocks, or one of the leading runners: that wasn't my way. It was my instinct to get overlooked, make myself anonymous. My check number suited me down to the ground—I preferred it to my name. Secrecy was second nature to me; either this or the most naked exposure. Anything competitive, like the survival-of-the-fittest race for the buses, and I was ready to drop out at the slightest excuse. I was solo. This flaw had to be protected, so I took elaborate precautions as a matter of instinct. If I was speaking to somebody and they spoke in a rough lingo, dropping aitches and so on, I did likewise. I liked to blend, please, agree, observe, listen sympathetically, if possible without having to contribute. I longed to contribute, pour myself happily without a thought, but I was beginning to sense treachery everywhere. And I was still speechless. That was why I had to keep quiet—I was growing a tongue. I took to it even as a kid, this merging: now I could do it with ease. It was the next best thing to being invisible. A woman said once to a friend of mine, ' Isn't he quiet—like a girl!'

14

I WAS solo, yet little by little over the years I was making contact with the odd pal here and there; nothing deep, but the ones I did make clung, for some reason. Nobody seemed to be trying, no effort, and most of these contacts belonged in the factory, that's all. I preferred it that way, took care to cultivate them in such a way that they wouldn't continue outside. Living at Lillington cut me off clean from them as soon as I jumped on my bike and bent over the handlebars. Back in the city again I tried, without being unfriendly, to keep my free hours solitary. That wasn't so easy. I was saved by their girls, mostly. Al Fillimore had a girl, he was a young apprentice fitter working nearby when I was on the lathes, and I often found myself biking home with him through the streets: he lived in my direction. He had hard red curls that seemed to cling to his forehead, and he clung to me in the same way, like a hard growth that was nothing to do with him personally. He was bright, younger than me, nervy and alert, charming with a touch of moodiness, and he affected an indifference that was either jeering or bored, bored like a boy walking in puddles, or the nearest he could get to the casual look he adored in his heroes. These were all singers, famous names, Americans. His face was freckled. He walked slightly hunched because he had one arm shorter than the other. A jellybaby, he did a tough guy act. You only had to fumble, search for words and he'd let you have it : ' If you've got nothing to say, shut up!' I liked him, liked his nutty humour, his plump bouncy body, but after a while he unnerved me, made me restless. He was easier to be with, more relaxed, when he was with his girl Francie, a young blonde he was courting, who acted the tomboy and played his stooge, wisecrack for wisecrack, but under the fun and games meant business. And under his fooling and oh so casual air, he was a bit wary. I saw them rowing once in the street—she'd been kept waiting a few minutes. ' You're late,' she said, and before he could open his mouth, off she flounced up the street, white-faced, furious. He put on the indifferent act for my benefit, but I saw the score.

So there was him, mad on the big bands, rolling his eyes and saying ' Jesus!' and giving his imitation through the hole in his fist, using it as a trumpet for those frenzied last riffs, when the brass riots. And his Judy Garland, Sinatra, Ella. Naturally it had to be Yank, the English were wet as a can of piss. He'd sit listening to records he'd brought round, and there was no point in him listening, he had every note off by heart, every inflexion. Come to think of it, he only half listened, grinning and twitching his hips, having a boyish nibble at his girl's neck, saying in a stage whisper with a wink in my direction, ' Let's go snogging tonight,' and she'd say, ' Don't say that word, it's horrible!'

There were others, more stodgy, scattered about in different departments, and they might hail me if I was wandering past, say to the stores, or I'd walk over to their position deliberately for a quick chat. Mostly they'd be fellow apprentices, but there was one older bloke—old enough to be my father—I'd got to know years before, when I was on the lathes. He was a veteran, a skilled turner. In idle moments when I worked on his gang I used to watch him, the great hoops of cast iron he had to manhandle into his chuck, his face tense with effort, yanking over the wooden crossbar to start his old machine, winding up the saddle with one hand and to save a couple of seconds giving the turret a final yank with the wrench as it slid in to the attack. From morning to night he seemed like that, in a mad rush. I worked on an even older machine, a real

wreck, right behind him. For some reason I never understood he befriended me, if you could call it that, and years
later I couldn't go down his gangway without him calling
me over to ask how I was. He couldn't stop working to
have a yarn, even for a couple of minutes, and his moan
was always the same: the time allowed on the job he was
doing, whatever it happened to be, was too short. They'd
undercut him, the only way he could make it pay was by
flogging himself to death. ' I'd be stupid to do that,
wouldn't I? What do you think?' He thrashed about in a
fury, twisting his head at me to make sure I hadn't escaped,
his face charred and contorted, now and then a ghastly
smile lighting it up like a neon sign: on, off.

' The bleeders,' he'd pant, ' look at the time they've
given me on this lot; I've got to do so-and-so '—and he'd
reel off a string of processes ' and how much time for each?
Eh? Eh? Have a guess, go on. The fuckers!'

He put the fear of God into me for some reason. I'd
stand by the side of him, my will paralysed, wanting desperately to shove off and racking my brains for an excuse.
He had a disconcerting habit of shooting out a personal,
direct question, and his eyes bored into you and there was
no escape. Once he rasped out, wiping his hands on a wad
of cotton waste:

' Know how old I am? Have a guess.'

He dug his forefinger into the mess of Russian fat and
daubed the bright points of his centres. I made some
attempt, but what he was working round to was how old
my old man was. He had a nasty buttonholing approach if
he wanted information. All the years I knew him, he didn't
once use my name.

' Hey,' he'd call out, as you went slipping by hopefully,
' come here.'

' Okay?' I said, pausing, trying to look friendly and
harassed at the same time.

' What you got to tell me, then?'

' Nothing really . . .'

' What's the rush?'

' No rush.'

And he'd keep smiling, his bitter burning eyes fixed on

me, the smile like a rat-trap, gleaming, ferocious. 'What's the rush?' he'd repeat, eager and demanding, seeing me itching to be off. And the next move I knew by heart: his hand went up and grabbed the bar, tugged it violently and the machine stopped. He kept going, though, wiping the bed of his lathe, stripping down the turret, retooling, while he cross-examined me. This was his idea of a friendly chat. He kept it up for ten minutes, then all at once lost interest, the tempo of work increased, he had the chuck spinning and it was obvious he couldn't wait for you to push off. But if you went before he was ready, it was as if he was suffering pangs of jealousy.

'What's new then? What you got to tell me?'

'Oh, nothing . . . nothing much.'

'Must be something. Eh?'

'Can't think what.'

'Dad okay? Your mother?'

Or he might want an errand running. He begged, and pushed his face close, and his abjectness was so aggressive and resentful, jerked out, it made him uglier than ever. He hated me for doing him a good turn, even before I'd agreed to it. He'd rattle out harshly, like an accusation:

'Do me a favour?'

'Yes, sure.'

'Now hang on—not so fast—you don't know what it is yet.'

'No, alright . . .'

'Eh—eh?

'Listen, it's nothing, nothing much, I'd do it myself, you know that, but this bastard job—up to the bleedin' eyes in it I am—you understand? You can see for yourself can't you how I'm fixed. Anybody can if they ain't blind. Working my balls off, I am.'

'That's alright, I'll go.'

'If it's any trouble, tell me. Don't want to put you out.'

'No trouble.'

I'd set off, and he'd bawl down the gangway after me, 'Hang on—what about my check number? Know it by heart?'

Usually it was a trip to the stores, say to take a drill

back. Hand it over the top of the fence to the storekeeper, who dropped it in the bin and looked for the check number stamped on the brass checks hanging on the row of cup hooks. The check I could return any time I was passing, ' don't come back specially this way, understand,' but I took it straight back and dropped it on his tin workstand while the visit was still fresh. That way I avoided the risk of another long session, later. If we had a chat, he had to nab me on the trot past, and most weeks I was lucky, his head was well down. His hands grubbed and clawed, nails split, clogged with muck and oil, he was driven by time, the bastards in the office kept undercutting him and he went faster and still made the price pay. He'd show the bastards! They wouldn't grind him down. Nil desperandum illegitimo carborundum. He was more miserly than they were, and tougher. Case-hard. He lowered his cindery hard head, his ravaged face, sore eyes. Bitter, chippy. What did we have in common? Yet he had a soft spot for me.

The checks—I thought I'd forgotten those yellow discs stamped with my number, tokens of myself, perforated with the little hole near the edge so that they hung, mute and waiting, on the rows of cup hooks. They shine out now like suns! They're medallions round my neck, glorified by the years. The grey, tetchy old men stood at the wire fence waiting their turn irritably, a clock ticking away in their heads, the price of the job burning on their lined foreheads, and these brass bits would be between their fingers. They clutched them like misers, and the grim, purposeful middle-aged skilled men, the aristocrats, jingled them in their hands like easy money, the kids spun them up, tossed them, dropped them on the floor—the raw kids who, according to legend, were sent on those phoney errands to ask for rubber hammers, left-handed screwdrivers, bubbles for spirit levels, boxes of half-inch holes, tins of elbow grease.

I have no mastery, no cold skill, no deliberate craftsmanship and never will have; more and more I trust in the song. They had a saying, those skilled men, to register their contempt for fumblers like me : they said ' He couldn't fit my arse to a bucket.' Now I am able to handle tools in a dull common-sense manner, out of necessity. When it comes

G

to writing I'm at the mercy of moods. Then it's pure song or nothing, joy or painful, futile and dragging labour, senselessly cut off from my fellows; nothing in between. When it moves it pours and flashes, gallops, and all I do is name and name, convey a long-buried feeling, capture the truth, yet not for the truth's sake—truth goes by the board —but racing to keep up with the song. Who cares if somebody's waiting for a letter, if your socks stink, if your piles are bleeding? You sing. The singing becomes an end in itself (Listen to him, he thinks he can sing!). The joy of creation is the sudden haemorrhage. The Venus vein bursts, a blue stain appears on the back of the hand, a terrifying lump as long as an egg. You're so numb with shock you can't write. Instead you rush round to the doctor, bang on his door, interrupt his surgery: this is an emergency— might be a thrombosis. Push it under his nose, frantic— 'What is it?' All he does is glance at it in the half light through a crack in the door—the patients in his surgery craning their necks, flapping their ears—and snaps 'It's nothing, control yourself! Drink the medicine, it'll go away.' Go back to naming, staring at the stain. Tattoo-mark of creation—heaven emptied, draining away. Naming. Trust in that. ('When I write potatoes, I mean potatoes'.) The fading stain accuses all your struggles and toe-holds.

I was with the surface grinders when I sent Marion the note. She was a stocky little typist who worked somewhere in the offices at the front. I hadn't spotted her in there, it was her jaunty promenades every two or three days though the shop I'd seen, watching her through the thickets of machines and flapping belts with frightened eyes. I wasn't frightened of *her*, it was the action I contemplated, the web of circumstances I'd begun to spin, the fearful shyness of a youth who was all arrogance underneath, sickened by the sight of myself being rebuffed—I imagined it in detail, like a suicide about to jump who looks down and sees his shattered limbs down there on the pavement. She wore a white shirt-blouse, high lacy collar, a springy bubble-cut hair-do, her eyes were bright and mischievous, kept rigidly downcast most of the time on account of the wolf whistles.

Her fresh cheeks were flushed and childish. But it was her walk that got me, jaunty and eager for life. She bounced through the machine shop, gay and resilient as a rubber ball. I didn't have a crush on her—it was a matter of seizing the opportunity. There was a woman somewhere waiting for me, and who knows, it might be this one; if you didn't ask, how did you find out? The very thought of making a date with a girl vanquished me, but my mates did it all the time. And I'd reached such a pitch now, it was either her or prostitutes. I was on the point of going to London, just getting on a train and travelling there, solitary, waiting till it was dark and then standing there in one of those canyons behind Piccadilly till I was picked up. I'd mapped it out in my head a hundred times, how to turn myself into a he-man. But it wasn't sex I thought of when I saw Marion bouncing through, it was a breeze, a fresh breeze I felt. Her name ought to have been Jackie—something crisp and boyish. I saw her romantically as a bundle of life. And she issued from wonderland, crisp as a carol, clean and bright and shining. As a green apprentice, queuing in the spotless corridor at the front on Thursdays outside the Wages window, peering in at the purity of desks and dazzle of paper, the slick dandified staff, I felt a queer dizzy sensation—something like Alice in Wonderland. My brother was a clerk himself, but I never connected him with this Thursday vision. I was utterly in awe of her world.

Getting to know her cured that. The smiling face and nothing behind it—this was my first experience. The great thing was, I'd made the date, screwed myself up tight and gone up sweating, guts churning, and kept the appointment: an initiation ceremony. Meeting a girl. Girl. The very word was enough to make me stutter. You can always tell the ones who never have to struggle. They have a bored air, they never know the depths and the heights. I came away from that meeting dazed with marvels—and to think that I'd created such a moment by my own initiative! Everything had been against me—a non-mixer, non-dancer, working in a community of one sex just like a prison or a monastery. I'd overcome all that, and it's true that I had to wait years to get desperate for such effrontery. That's what it seemed, effrontery. Who passed in the note? I can't remember. It must have been someone I knew well and could trust, someone who knew her name so I could write ' Dear Marion '—flaming, fateful words—and could get it passed in to her without any trouble. ' Dear Marion, you won't know me. Would you like to meet me outside the main gate at ten to two this dinnertime?' Hardly inviting, and how could she see it was written in blood? Somehow it got passed back to me, with a smile of secrecy and a wink, and it was my own note back again, with one word scrawled across it. YES.

Close up she wasn't so hot, ignorant and a hint of a cast in one eye. She came up smiling, with that bouncy little walk which had freshened me, gave me a false impression of innocence. Close up she was more vacant than innocent, but sizing things up quick enough for all that.

' Hallo!' she said. ' How did you know my name?'

On the defensive already, I muttered : ' Somebody told me.'

' Somebody I know?'

We were getting near the gates, coming in. Forcing every breath, I asked her for a date.

' When?'

' Say Thursday night.'

Her eyes shining with triumph, she pretended to think.

' I can't Thursday. I wash my hair Thursdays.'

' Friday then.'

Again the hesitation, the little catlike smile. ' What time?' she said cautiously, because she'd only just met me and I might be anybody and if she said yes too quick, people would think she was loose.

Inside, nobody said anything, no one was aware of my transformation. Perhaps after all it wasn't visible. My head was whirling with impressions, and that afternoon went like a dream, as they say. I'd made a fool of myself, my voice had wavered at the crucial moment, and I re-enacted the idiotic little scene again and again, and all the time, gradually, I was beginning to let the truth about her register, enter through the cracks, a fragment at a time maybe, but the truth. Her voice, for instance, doing that coy dolly act. The cat-and-mouse game she played with me, and the look of cunning that flitted across her face at the mention of Thursday. Still, none of that mattered because I'd done it, I'd won, I was out—and I bowed my head lower, feeling the smile spreading and shining on my face like something indecent.

15

I was out, I sparkled. The thought of what I'd done shocked me, and if the daring hadn't been suspect, if I hadn't known how I'd been driven, it would have delighted me too. Being out meant I had to go on; I'd started something. To hell with that, for the moment I was out and free, standing there unsuspected, my boat pitching happily as it saw the open sea. I'd show those lover boys! It was like coming away from the dentist, no appointments, wandering down the pavement so blithe, head full of gibberish. A cloud in trousers. Only cowards know what paradise is. I got in a funk and it drove me to act and the anguish was worse. Suddenly you came out of the tunnel of fear into the pastures of heaven. Or you did it in reverse, tore yourself out of the buttercup field and went in. Like Dolphin Road School, grim as a reformatory, tramping up the stone stairs in a bunch, nameless, one of the damned, to the great barn of a room stinking of gas from the leaking taps where we coupled up the rubber tubes and lit the bunsen burners: home the other side of the world, my mother waving goodbye as I climbed on my bike and rode blindly, hopelessly away, sickened by the sight of the homely, crumbling infant and elementary school I had to pass at the bottom of our street, horrified by the rigour of the buildings, faces, crossings, all intent on delivering me to the hated place. And you thought as it closed round you, over and round, sucking, as you stepped into the prison yard for the first time and older kids ran up to try and flog you their old atlases, you thought you hated your parents for making you come to this place, you felt the pain and grief of their dreadful betrayal. A line of kids were playing that game where one boy ducked over double, his back horizontal and his hands braced against the brick wall, and another boy ran up and landed on his back. Then a rush of bodies, heads ducking like mad, backs bending, legs set apart and the one behind with his head wedged in your crotch and kids leap-frogging and landing every other minute on this long living horse of groaning backs. A blast of the whistle and the horse shuddered, then broke in the middle. Everybody scrambling off and running to form queues. Another whistle blast and we went shuffling in over the worn stone doorstep. The master was waiting for us at the top of the stairs. A giant in baggy trousers, with a fierce head of hair, bad teeth and black horn-rimmed glasses. He rolled the whites of his eyes, waited calmly for dead silence and then told us what would happen to us if we acted the fool instead of paying attention. He called the register. The strange names flowed, mine among them, and when he reaches the name Shelley, this boy, John Shelley, answers 'Here sir' with such lazy confidence or indifference that I can't believe I've heard right. The master doesn't pay any attention. I stared at this boy's head, at the back of his neck, in a kind of wonder and adoration. It was all right, I was going to get out of here, I'd go flying home through the streets tonight, nobody was going to touch me, nothing was going to happen while John Shelley was here. He was my first hero at this terrible stealthy place. I didn't pal up with him. I loved him from afar; I trembled for him, held my breath over him. Right from the beginning he seemed to attract wrath, without even trying: it was just his nature. He stuck up in the air and glittered with unconscious opposition, inviting the storm like a lightning conductor. He got warned repeatedly, hauled out and caned again and again, then he'd be absent for long sessions. We thought he was playing truant but he wasn't, he was ill of some obscure disease. In the end his parents took him away from that school.

That was when the dread reality gripped me, as we trooped in, a teacher herding us from the rear, and I put my feet on the bottom flight of those bare stone steps and saw how *hollowed-out* they were. I choked, something died inside me at the sight of that wear and permanence. I was being abandoned. Abandon hope all ye who enter here. Infant school was nothing, sweet piping songs like ' Away in a Manger ', those cosy ramshackle rooms with the crayon drawings tacked up, a big framed picture of Jesus behind glass bidding the little children to come unto Him, and there they were sitting in a circle at His feet, warm and close, all races, and He was in the middle, an effulgent, gentle, feminine figure, His head bathed in rosy light and His hands resting on the heads of the two nearest children and it was plain to see they trusted Him, loved Him . . . Miss Warren it could have been, teaching us to sing D'ye Ken John Peel, every now and then stoking up the round pot-bellied stove with more coke, rattling the bucket and tilting it and ramming the shovel under the stubborn coke energetically till she had a shovelful. I used to love the wintry sound of it. Then she'd pick up the steel hook and catch hold of the glowing lid and flip it open, we saw the red flames licking and leaping, in flew the coke and that was that. Maybe she'd give the ashes a shake through the grille at the bottom, jabbing a long poker through the bars. It was winter, the air sparkled outside the windows. You could see the adverts being changed on the wall of Fredman's sports shop, the billposter's ladder waving about and then the bloke climbing up in full view, a bag of posters slung round his neck, the bucket of paste in one hand and wide, long-handled brush in the other. Once he waved to us, the ones who saw him waved back excitedly and the teacher said if it happened again she'd draw the curtains. That was crabby old Miss Vercoe who took handicrafts, she was deaf and chalky, veins like fat worms on the backs of her hands, she shouted and lost her temper, but what was that now? I longed for her so much it was like a pain, I wanted her and the long whiskers growing out of her chin and Jesus on the wall and the filthy washhouse where we washed the inkwells and milk bottles, I wanted Joe Buckley coming at me in the playground with his shaved head down on his shitty jumper, his arms flailing like windmills, I wanted the shithouse where the same yellow porcelain trough ran under all the seats and boys at one end made paper boats and set fire to them and tried to make them sail along under your innocent little arse shining so white and moony. And dancing round the maypole, spiralling the white tapes, skipping round joyous as lambs, boys and girls together. No bitter gulf between school and home. You played with fag cards against the school wall, out in the street, you sat on the pavement skimming the cards and feeling sharp pangs of loss if you got beaten, and it was the same pavement outside your own house, just down the street. Everything was joined on, continuous. You played marbles in the gutter, going nearly all the way home like that, measuring and aiming and rolling the magic striped glass, eyes glued to the cobbles, and the gutter ended at the drain under the lamp-post opposite the entry which sliced down the side of your house. Now it was changed, it was strange and terrible. Dolphin Road ran parallel with Albert Road—a slow hill ending at a common. Dinnertimes I went slinking up to the common with my sandwiches, and sat in a crab-apple tree right over near the far edge, nearest the factories. I perched there morbidly, a pale ninny, a painted bird, and the weak sunlight pecked at me, or the drizzle, and it was all the same to me in my misery. I was lost in the void.

To begin with it was only the emptiness, the strangeness, the bigness, and of course the distance—travelling right into and through the town, along Ford Street, Corporation Street, glancing at the out-of-date film posters outside the Rex on a Monday and being stabbed and sickened by the reminder of that lost week-end. Lob End, Butchers' Row, Broomfield. It was a different town that side from the one you thought you knew. The emptiness didn't have a name so how could you tell your parents, how could you beg them to stop it? If you could have found words for it you'd have said *worn steps, worn steps*! They'd have said don't be silly, it's because you're new there and don't know any-body, don't be so daft making such a fuss, what a cry-baby. Can you understand him? they'd say to each other. My mother would ask why, why did I have such a difficult child. I worry myself sick over you—you'll be the death of me. Earlier it was rage, the chase with the copper stick—

I'll swing for you. Now it was all worry. So I kept the emptiness hidden, and then I'd catch my mother looking sideways at me and the helpless misery in her face, the foolish fluttering inadequacy and fear of the truth were so plain I knew she'd got it too, the emptiness. I'd passed it on. My father was immune, his schooldays had been all right, but my mother had endured the same nameless reign of terror. She could tune in to any frequency if there was suffering in it. She couldn't help herself. Behind her eyes was the secret life of real nightmares that couldn't ever be brought out into the open and acknowledged for what they were. To do that meant action, opposition, it meant fighting back. How could you fight Them? All my mother could do was endure and suffer, weep inside, bear another cross. One more. If you came near that truth behind the eyes, as I did accidentally later, she got panicky and squawked like a terrified bird, cried *Stop it!* and as a last resort turned on the tap or threw a fit of hysterics. Nobody dragged the truth out in our house after a while, it was too nerve-racking.

The sense of desolation wasn't something you could perhaps get used to, like in prison—it renewed itself with fresh force every Monday because you'd buried yourself away from it in the week-end, as a kid buries its face in its mother's apron, to shut out the truth. And the longer the escape, the more harrowing the journey back. The long summer holidays were the worst, and Christmas, when you noticed bitter reminders of happiness in people's houses, the paper chains still hung across the ceiling, the decorated Christmas trees on show in the front windows. A howling started deep inside you and you bit your lips and kept your mouth shut tight, to keep the howl soundless.

I idolised John Shelley. There was another John who was a godsend to me—John McGough—though I didn't idolise him, I pitied him. He was an object of pity. That was a blessing and a comfort, having somebody in the class you could pity. When I realised he was as immune to pity as he was to insults I started to love him. He was my anchor. At the first mental test he sank to the bottom, natural as a stone. He was bottom each term, stuck in the front row so the teacher could keep an eye on him. He was naturally dopey and naturally good-natured. He wasn't lazy, he worked and concentrated and struggled to do better. I prayed for him not to improve because if he hadn't occupied that bottom position I'd have been there. The disgrace of that bottom place was rubbed out by the mere fact of him being there in occupation. It belonged to him, you felt, in the natural order of things: that was how it was meant to be. That was because John McGough was so blissfully stupid, he had no sense of shame, he blinked round and grinned amiably when the results were read out as if to say 'That's all right then.' I liked him best of anybody in that class. He lived out on the rural fringe of the city, up a rutted earth lane, and the chaotic farmhouse interior of his home bewildered me. I liked it though. So that was it, I kept saying to myself, he was a farm boy, a country boy! His mother and his home, the whole disorderly set-up was exactly in character, vague and open-mouthed and easy-going, amiably sluttish. I went home with him one night and we were supposed to do our homework together, sitting at the big scrubbed table with the oil lamp in the middle. 'I shouldn't bother any more,' his mother kept saying, slopping about in her ragged slippers, smiling indulgently at the two of us. 'I should pack up now if I were you.' Cats lay about, snoozing, and there was a dog scratching its fleas.

At the other end of the classroom, sitting in the back row in a corner against the wall, were the two stars. The teacher didn't need to keep his eye on them so they were right out of reach, a law unto themselves: they could be trusted to work swiftly and well and give no trouble. They were embryo teachers anyway. Before you could finish one set of problems these two were sitting up straight with arms folded, bland smiles on their faces as they waited for more. They were so detestable to me that I didn't even consider them as kids in the sense that John McGough was a kid. I remember particularly and vividly the buttery smiles spreading on their chops. They were adults already, pompous, assured, they were greased with cleverness, noses sharp with achievement, they couldn't get out of their childhoods fast enough. They spread their legs and leaned back in the narrow iron-framed desks, cramped by the simplicities of this world I found so hard to absorb. On the sports field it was the same story, it revolved round them, they were the stars and it was too simple for words, a game you could play with your eyes shut. They were killing time, those two. One of them, Clive Adrian, went on to play soccer for England.

Nicknames: Flash Harris, Whacker Payne, Gabby Rogers. There was something icy and ominous, crackling and electric about the teachers at that school. Then we moved from the big ugly workhouse pile at Dolphin Road to a modern, glass-and-wood low-level building at Whitelanes, near Albany Road and Stanley Avenue, not far from the iron bridge at Stanley Park and the railway junction, the goods yard, the panoramic view over the city if you jumped so that your head bobbed over the grey steel ramparts of the bridge, studded with rivets; and over there were the spires, Monkswell Green, the first world war tank, huge and stranded and prehistoric, squatting lifeless on the clipped turf in the midst of the flower beds. Whitelanes, and going home I used to push up the avenue to the top, standing on the pedals and crunching the gravel, to the posh grammar school on the corner of the main road, avenues of chestnuts, traffic flowing and the posh kids lounging on the corner, by their decorative spiked gates and warm stone and castellated ivy-covered walls.

Whitelanes. The reign of terror really began for me there, when I found myself at Whitelanes with Chirpy Birdsall. He was my new form teacher. He wasn't bald, but his hair was fair, stuck down on his large bladdery head, which gave an impression of baldness. I dreaded him so much I was afraid to hate him even, in case he sensed the hatred welling out of me. He was the kind of teacher who had antennae for picking up things like that. He exuded an atmosphere—I can't describe it in any other way. He didn't pick on me personally, he used the cane brutally and indiscriminately. He was plump and smooth and pitched his voice low, in fact it was an affectation of his, this unruffled, leisurely, cool approach. His head swayed as he walked, and even sitting at his desk marking our books, his head down, I seemed to feel the same deadly snakelike presence about to strike. He only had to come into the room and flick his grey eyes over us to terrorise me. The bond between the torturer and his victim is more intense and close than between lovers, they say. All I know is that years later, when I'd got right away from him and could have come back and spat in his eye if I'd wanted, I was buying suede shoes and a tweed sports jacket in imitation of him.

I must have been more than desperate, I must have been half out of my mind with fear and anxiety to do what I did in the end on account of that devil. Imagine it, forging the initials of a man who could make you palpitate like the sides of a mouse trapped in a bucket if he strolled up behind you and just paused a minute. My loathing was close to worship, he inspired such grovelling panic. And I did it, my ratlike, slithering, beady terror started me on a career of petty crime—I forged his initials, F.B., in red ink on the bottom of the page of homework I couldn't finish.

Mild and almost bored, he called me out. There was my crime, shaking letters, square and squat but seismographic, too thin, too dry, no oil of smoothness. The lazy inquisition:

' What's this?'

' What sir?'

' This.'

' It's . . . it's . . .'

' That's not my writing, now is it?'

' Yes, sir.'

' No seriously.'

' Yessir!'

' You honestly expect me to believe that I wrote that? Is that my F? Now I ask you.'

' Yessir!'

Murmuring and languorous: ' I must have been drunk, that's all I can say . . .' then the jaw snapping: ' You did it, didn't you?'

' No sir!'

' Sure?'

' Yessir!'

And the fantastic moment when he sighed: ' All right. Go back to your place.' How I loved him in a daze of worship and wonder, how I suffered at the deception, those barefaced lies I told him. Now I wanted to take them all back. I would have owned up if I'd known he was going to be human and let me off like that. My gratitude tormented me, and what I'm thinking now is, he may have intended exactly that. I wouldn't put anything past him, the slimy shit.

One day, as I've described elsewhere. I hung my satchel round my neck and climbed on my bike, waved good-bye to my mother and then, instead of riding off in the right direction I went round in a circle at the first turning, heading nowhere, belonging nowhere. I was playing truant, another crime, and again a seizure of acute anxiety had caused it, the unfinished homework in my satchel had forced great daring on me. The bike took me in the opposite direction from Whitelanes, into the country void beyond Sutton Common, around Alvington, the golf links, aerodrome, abbey. Now my abandonment and loneliness were absolute—this latest suicide act put a seal of secrecy on my movements. There was nobody I could tell. Riding, wandering, sitting, stationary with one foot on a grass bank to prop me up, so I could stay hunched lifeless on the saddle and wait, wait for the time to pass, I'd dream of the places that were like impossible idylls now, saturated with welcome and love and cheerfulness, places of early childhood I'd taken for granted at the time: Ashmoor, Carroll Green, Belle Vue Gardens. Flowery, summery, heart-breaking names. Ashmoor and the Alpine—only five miles out but thrilling, foreign land, past the pit and its mining village, a few ugly rows of terraces in the middle of nowhere, the bleak waste of the kids' playground, gaunt bones of swings sticking up, chains rattling, the iron wheel of the roundabout and its stump rooted in the concrete. Out into no-man's land and a looming mountainous slag-heap, colliery wheels, then the country. Scrub land, miniature precipices, the lane in shadow, overhung by big, perched rocks, the biggest I'd seen, slabs of sandstone covered with bushes and saplings, with goat paths worn by the feet of hundreds of kids who came out to scramble all over its lumps and crevices. The cleft of the lane between banks of clay; sudden panorama at the top by the church and the wooden post office. Foreign land—different altogether from the direction I knew, the rolling watermeadows and flat fields and leafy parkland of Orford, Charlcott, Wellsbourne, Stratford, and on to Evesham and its orchards, fruit stalls along the grass verges, Pershore and the soft slow river ambling under the feathery willows, striped fish in the muddy waters . . .

Ashmoor was different. I stayed with Uncle Mike and Aunt Olive, they had a bungalow—nothing on one side, on the other a space, then a lonely-looking semi-detached and its twin, like town houses that had lost their street, then another vacant strip next to a wooden bungalow, and at the bottom of the slope another towny house that was the Stores. The bell tinkled, the floor was bare planks, all the stuff was fly-blown, nobody came to serve for a long time and a baby cried in the back. There was no proper village; a garage, a blacksmith. The Rising Sun. Uncle Mike's bungalow had nothing at the back except the raw heath, his own big lawn ending at a trellis, behind that some vegetables and then a field of rough grass, his, where he had pigs, and in the middle of it, among the pits of earth where the pigs had rooted, stood a full-size dirty bell tent. Inside were more holes dug by the pigs, rotten cabbages, torn newspaper, candle-ends. And at the front of the bungalow was a flower bed and a patch of lawn and a stone fence, somehow forlorn and pointless, and beyond it just the empty lane and a thorn hedge and then nothing; the scrub land of the heath, only a few acres but it was wild and seemed huge, with no hedges, owned by nobody, going up and down under the clouds and kestrels, a dour solitude. We called it the Moor.

Carroll Green was forlorn like Ashmoor, yet it was barely over the boundary, on the fringes; in fact the double-decker buses ran out to there and turned round. It was stagnant, emptied, neither town nor country. I went with my brother sometimes in the long summer holidays for a fortnight, staying with another uncle and aunt. They lived in a brick house like a council house, and it was creepy in a nice sort of way, grassy verges instead of pavements, hardly any traffic, and like Ashmoor there would be special nights when you heard a funny hooting sound or a hand bell ringing; the fish-and-chip van on Fridays, the hardware, Wednesday morning, and the grocery came on Monday afternoon and often it was late. Dennis and Caroline were young, not long married, with no children then. Dennis would come in after work at night, softly enter the room, smile at us, murmur something friendly and go and say soft caressing things to his moody young wife, who welcomed him sentimentally, slushily, as if he was coming home from a long campaign abroad. It was good when he came in, the morbid atmosphere from Caroline ebbed away. If it was chilly he fetched sticks and stooped down at the grate and soon kindled a fire. He was a maintenance man at the pit; small, lean, fine-boned, with a gaunt handsome face—I loved the pallor, the fine stubble on his cheeks —and hair brushed straight back, springy, going bald at the bony white temples. He was gifted musically, played the piano in a dance band. In the evenings he used to sit humming softly to himself and tapping his foot. Even for work his shoes were as pointed and dandyish as his patent leather dancing shoes. He was a gentle, vacillating character, his voice low and subtly modulated. He fascinated me. He had a presence, there was an actor in him somewhere. Because he'd been ill he used his own towel. Now and then he coughed a short dry cough, and he covered his mouth with his hand discreetly.

One thing happened at their place which tainted for ever that aura of innocence. I was in the long grass in the field at the back with my brother, we had our flies open and were satisfying our curiosity, examining each other. Caroline came up suddenly and surprised us. Without a word she turned away and went back in. There was never any reference to the incident. It was just unmentionable as far as she was concerned—like the time I was staying at the caravan with Pearl, running up the steps and barging in as she was standing there stark naked, about to pull on her bathing costume. I couldn't take it in, it was unearthly, like something off another planet. Afterwards I found it impossible to remember any details of that awful revelation, only a blur of flashing whiteness and hair where it shouldn't have been. Hair somewhere. Ginger. Auntie Pearl wasn't ginger. I thought I'd dreamt it, it happened so quick.

Now at the factory the thing had a name, a woman had a hairy twat or a quim or a fanny between her legs, and it was referred to with violence and harsh contempt by the lads of my own age, as if it had a life of its own, and though they made a pretence of lusting after this impersonal twat it seemed to me they really feared and hated it. The malevolence would be transferred to the person, whoever she was. ' Look at her, the bitch—her quim's been reamed so often you wouldn't even touch the sides.'

And the jokes were the same, a mixture, often brutal, of disgust and fear and desire—like the one about the woman who baulked at the sight of her lover's erection, which was like a stallion's. So she told him to tie a handkerchief half-way up before he started, she'd take half and no more, understand? When he was on the job the handkerchief fell off and he sank his great cock in up to the hilt. ' That's fine,' she said. ' Now you can give me the other half.'

This wasn't a joke of the apprentices—none of them were—but they picked on ones that appealed to them as expressions of their uneasiness. In their mouths, in the telling, it acquired the qualities they needed to pass on, for the horse laugh of reassurance. After all, they hadn't set eyes on a fanny, most of them, any more than I had. In our imaginations it got bigger and bigger until it threatened to suck us in, boots and all, like Jonah lost in the whale.

If a man was randy, on heat, courting—this wasn't our expression either—they said he had two cocks, one in each pocket. But the last word in factory abuse, man or boy, would be literally that word cunt. ' Silly twat!' they'd hurl at you. ' Useless cunt!' Or, cold and flat, the insult to end insults, delivered full in the face : ' You cunt.'

And this disembodied, useless, evil, stupid, winking hole,

hung up in public and derided, spat at, it could jump into you like a bug and spread and fester and erupt. It was cancerous, it was cataclysmic. You were whole, then the next minute the fabric split from top to bottom, the dream of bread and circuses was over, the vicious war was on, peace shattered and stinking. A greasy gravy of sex dripped on the sheets. The clear cuntless eyes of childhood grew a trembling glaucoma, the innocent light dimmed and got membranous, a sort of murky twilight that thickened all day and turned into a hairy darkness at night, choking out the sun. In dirty photos it was unspeakable, a filthy brown sink-hole, stained and wrinkled, ugly as hell. Unthinkable that your mother, your sister had one. It was an untouchable, unmentionable wound opening in your mind. It sank into you, burned deep into your thoughts and took root there, scabby, inflamed, festering. No peace now—the sauce bottle shot its load, the bread was flesh-white and clinging.

The bread. I'm thinking now of that fabulous childhood bread, lily-white in our grubby fingers. ' Eric's got a piece —please Mum can I have a piece?' Eric Gaskell from next door, only the other side of the entry, but their garden fence was high-boarded, trellis on top of that and rambler roses woven in and out, impregnable as a fort. He let me go in and play on their oblong of lawn, which was perfect like a tablecloth. Very conscious of the compliment, I'd go in almost on tiptoe, on my best behaviour. We'd squat there intent, grave as old men, manoeuvring a red-painted toy crane, winding the hook up and down. The handle had a cog and ratchet and the clicking sound it made excited us. Once when everybody was out he took me indoors, and I can see him now in the pantry at the back of the kitchen— and see myself goggling at him in amazement, he was such a clean, superior, subdued boy—drinking milk straight out of the milk jug.

Either him, or somebody you really loved, say Ronnie Hooper—waiting at the end of the entry, a piece stuck in his hand. I'd get mine too and go bolting out with it joyfully, bouncing on up the road to the park or lolling at the next corner against the wall, munching those thick delectable slices of bread and jam, bread and dripping, bread and marg. Delicious, blissful, melting in the mouth because you were eating it with your best-loved friend in freedom, away from the table, in the open air with nobody watching, and you could smear the jam over your clock and wipe your mouth on your sleeve and let crumbs drop and that was part of the feast, the special flavour came from that fact of not being under anyone's eagle eye. No adults. Sauntering on up towards the park, rolling the tongue around for stray fragments, smacking your lips exaggeratedly, still enjoying the taste in retrospect long after the last crumb had gone.

Ronnie Hooper's toast, or rather the toast made at his house, that was even more ambrosial. He was my best friend when we were six or seven years old. I don't remember his homely mother, she's shadowy and so is her living-room, but I can still see and taste the toast she made. If we ever had toast at our house it was done in a rush; either burnt, wedge-shaped, unevenly cooked or falling to bits. Something was usually wrong with it. Ronnie Hooper's mother toasted the square even slices with a kind of ritualistic slowness, taking down the fancy brass fork from its nail by the chimney breast, and she'd spear the bread on the prongs almost lovingly. She'd draw up a stool like a milkmaid and squat in front of the black-leaded range, the fire bright red behind the little vertical grille, just right. The half-softened butter was on a saucer in the grate, ready, and it went on generously, fat solid nobs on the sizzling gold. I was given a full piece, so was Ronnie, we'd smile at each other before tucking in, meek angels out of Dickens as we crouched on either side of the hearth.

16

STAFF of life. The parks—we lived in the parks, and at the top of Far Whatford Street, on the road out to Compton and Worsley Pit, we had a choice of three. Or we dirt-tracked around in the back entry, oblivious to the stink of sour milk and rotten meat, never looking once at the towering black bulk of the Humber building. I wonder now if I was imitating the speedway out at Compton when I went skidding round corners, digging in my heel to make the ashes fly, making the back wheel slide and slither—my father was a speedway fan, he took me out to the track one Saturday afternoon and I sat on his shoulders in the crush, getting the fierce tang of burnt petrol in my nose, terrified by the ear-splitting racket. Later, when scooters got too babyish and a soap-box trolley was the rage I nagged at somebody to make me one. Then it was a matter of finding the right spot, a quiet hill, a strip of deserted pavement and some means of slowing down at the bottom. This was the car world now, it was a car town where even the workers had cars of their own, so naturally we needed soap-box cars for playing in. You sat there in state on the plank and pram wheels, the axle swivelled under the feet by two cords which you held in your hands and tugged as if you held horse reins. On waste ground where the grass had been worn off it was a free, hectic, bumping ride, and on a gentle slope of pavement it was slow and oiled, majestic. Certain streets had special atmospheres. Hampton Street, for instance—long, quiet and gradual, ideal for a trolley, right near home, so you could nip out before tea was ready, straight after school, gliding down slowly, gathering speed, hearing the regular bump-bump as the cast iron covers of the pavement gutters ran under the wheels—at the bottom grabbing the reins and charging up again to the the top for just one more ride. And all the time you were conscious that it was a false, special, mysterious quietness, Hampton Street, with the rush-hour traffic increasing on either side in those parallel streams of Hyson Road and Whatford Street. It gave the street an atmosphere that was curious and enjoyable. To intensify the pleasure, the good fortune, the sheer luck of being there at all it was only necessary to sit still a second and listen to the faint rumble of traffic, steady as a battle.

I'm a street kid, now always and for ever, I live in the streets and back entries and waste bits, lurk in ambush at night, heart thumping, I listen with my whole body like an animal, the switched-off torch in my hand held like a gun.

I run with the pack, scream out when they do, utter blood-curdling yells to demoralise the enemy, race gasping for cover like a fugitive. Already I'm a little criminal, treacherous, audacious—the gang spirit rules me. When the light nights come, that puts an end to the mock battles and heroics, the violent hurtling chases; the gangs break up and we drift away on our own into the parks. These are waste bits to us, the grass foreign and interesting, funny stuff, we pluck at it as we sprawl around, taste it and chew on it like a food. Fields and even the common are places you go for treats and holidays, they don't count as real like the streets. The streets are our fields, our element—where the drama is. Things happen, even in Ernaldlhay Street. I'm running somewhere and a motorbike's handlebar catches me on the side of the head and knocks me out. They carry me into my own house, lay me on the settee in the front room where we only go at Christmas and this is summer, I wake up and find strange people staring down at me. Laughs of relief, ' He's alright, look, just grazed him, he's lucky you know—don't worry, Mrs.' They fetch a doctor and I have to lie down again, on the living-room table this time, while he prods and pushes and squeezes me like my mother making pastry. Not long before this I'd had my tonsils out on this very table, creeping downstairs in my pyjamas, and if I put my eye to the boards where there was a crack I could see the whole scene below me; the table spread with a rubber sheet, the bolster for my head, covered with the best towel, the doctor and his assistant and the mysterious equipment for giving me the gas, rubber mask and pipe, all ready and waiting, our living-room invaded. No escape.

The streets meant escape; nobody could grab you for anything. On Sundays if we were going on a visit to our grandparents, the route march began in the familiar home ground streets and was soon in the avenues, Terry Avenue, Humber Avenue, the long hill alongside the railway bank and the buttercup field up in the direction of the fever hospital. The houses drew back mockingly as we marched through, our parents guarding the rear. The exercise brought out my father's army training, never failed, he scowled and shouted at us to pick up our feet, warned us to pack up this or that, let out an irate bellow or two, and got choked off by our mother: 'John, you're shouting again.' This made his temper a little uglier, and by the time we reached our destination he was on the point of lashing out at us. It was too late, he couldn't touch us then. 'Wait till we get home,' he muttered, impotent, and we didn't feel threatened. Home was a long way off. At Belle Vue Gardens it was lovely, rural, we were spoiled and indulged and everything was in league with us; the bungalow made by the sons after the first war, with no building experience—a big raised veranda like something in America; the cess-pit, the bucket lavatory, the frogs, even the currant bushes. In the front was a billiard table and a tall cabinet of yellow wood stuffed with musty picture books and sheet music, chaotic; when the doors were opened, stuff on the top started sliding out as if it was alive. Through the small windows you could see raspberry bushes and fruit trees, the boughs nearly scraping the glass. The time blossomed, the green was heraldic and yet homely.

Belle Vue was a huddle of shacks in a hollow, dirt roads between, which were no more than wide bumpy tracks full of pot-holes; a slum community of factory workers, railway workers like my grandfather, working men with enterprise and no money who'd managed to buy a parcel of ground and build a bungalow. Some were no more than sheds, hovels—Geoff always cracked the joke about the woman in one of them who'd empty her pisspot out of the window with a grand gesture. He did it with actions, his arm shot out and his clenched fist twisted, tipping the invisible piss into the garden. You could almost see it fall in a curtain. His mother's bungalow was substantial, half brick and half asbestos, slates on the roof like a street house. Belle Vue lived in the shadow of factories, Austin and Humber, and in the heavier shadow of the city itself—and it was inside the boundary yet with its own trickle of traffic, its own pulse and circulation of news and doings, like a village.

On the machine grinders too it had the same feeling of being a family, a village, scruffy and shitty and overlooked by a miracle, caught in the steel guts of a whale that spouted youths and men; you travelled in and out on its breath, too insignificant to matter. We were a gang of five or six, with a chargehand who was supposed to keep an eye on us and iron out our problems, and as well as this he had his own quota of work to produce. From morning to night he went like the clappers, ever on the trot, sweating; that was his character. If Bert Ferguson walked up behind him and asked him if he could spare a minute, he'd keep jerking away frantically at the handles of his machine, his head screwed round to talk, stuttering apologetically that he'd be right there, yes, along in half a sec. ' If I can just finish this Bert—okay?' If he wasn't in a tearing hurry it was most peculiar, he didn't look natural at all. Paddy *scuttled*. His first name, Julian, had such dignity that you wanted to burst out laughing, it was so inappropriate. Everybody called him Pad, even the foreman Mr Gutteridge. He was obsequious, ludicrous, he scuttled backwards, forwards and sideways like a crab—but much faster, like an earwig in a fit. He was in a permanent sweat of panic and embarrassment, and seemed to have been born that way. He had the best and worst qualities of the Irish, eloquence and hypocrisy. The most contemptible and shameful thing about him from our point of view was that he was so obviously shitting himself. Nobody hated cowards—who isn't one himself?—but he made it so obvious to everybody, that was the disgusting thing. Because of this craven streak he scuttled harder and harder, trying to be nice and accommodating. He crept up your arsehole and laid eggs of goodwill in your bloodstream. He had sad, pale, saucer eyes and a blob of nose, like Dylan Thomas, only he was taller, a bone of a man, there was no fat on him and no sloth, he was all speed and anxiety. There was no arguing about his skill either, and he'd done it without the advantage of an apprenticeship, getting a foothold first as a semi-skilled millwright, accepting a lower rate than the others, then watching people and picking up tips, waiting to jump in as soon as there was a vacancy, licking arses too, of course, as hard as he could go. It was wonderful though, he'd do anything for you, anything to keep the work flowing smoothly, tearing up and down with his black hair falling into his eyes.

Mr Gutteridge was very pleased with him. If you were in trouble you yelled ' Pad !' and he'd come racing up, servile as a flunkey, spilling out his lovely vowels, putting every-thing right and shipshape in a flash with his quick clever fingers, his agile brain.

The machines we worked were in line astern, facing the same direction, Pad leading, with his back to us. Behind me was Bert Ferguson, behind him a youngster barely out of his time, George Holloway, and at the back of him another apprentice, Ginge Radcliffe. Ginge, or Wank—he'd collected this nickname from somewhere and it seemed to fit; I mean he looked as if he was the wanking type—had nothing to say to any of us. A tall, freckled streak, long camel neck and prominent Adam's apple, he was morose, broody, encased in silence. If he was asked some-thing point blank and forced to answer, he stared full at you, deadpan, with a venomous expression in his dark-ringed eyes that seemed calculated to curl you up. Occa-sionally I heard him blow up at the back of me, he'd made a mistake or the job on his magnet chuck had slewed round all of a sudden, or it was Monday and he was feeling more than usually savage. ' Bollocks, bollocks !' he'd howl, a favourite expression. He was gifted with a natural foul mouth, he swore coldly, with an icy vigour which made me flinch. Without the word fuck in his sentences he'd have been speechless. ' Got the fucking spanner?' he'd say, his arms dangling dangerously. Standing beside Bert Ferguson, a middle-aged, genial man, he'd ask him : ' Got the time you old fucker?'

George Holloway was the comic, he was corny, cheerful, laughed at his own jokes. His favourite stance at the machine was with one leg cocked like a dog taking a piss on the second shelf of his tin workstand. He'd twirl the chuck under his carborundum wheel and watch the showers of sparks, taking care and worrying but making it look very casual. He had a Lancashire comedian's accent but he wasn't funny, only by accident. I laughed in the right places, just to humour him. Ginge never bothered to hide his boredom. ' Got the tool?' he'd say, meaning the spanner for tightening the wheel nut.

'Yeah I got a smasher I 'ave, wanna see it?' George croaked, for the hundredth time.

'Stop bollockin' about, for fuck's sake,' Ginge gabbled, finding his voice for once. It was a half-choked boy's voice. Once I saw one of his rare smiles, his thick lips twisting up one side of his face before he could stop it. It was an exposure of that convulsive shyness he kept well buried. I looked the other way.

One day he disappeared, transferred to another section, and for a week or two his machine was vacant. Finally a skilled man, Freddy, turned up to replace him. What a contrast. He was voluble all right, and a performer so that he could be. He sang hymns, nothing but hymns, holding forth like a gospel soloist. Nobody knew why, as he was anything but religious. He gave a daily concert at the machine, warbling expertly and putting all the power of his lungs into the top notes, to everybody's embarrassment. We got used to it in the end and took no notice; there he was flinging his head back and airing his tonsils, and he wasn't even registering with us. Not a flicker. He could have been whistling, or his machine extra noisy—nobody turned their heads to look. That didn't exactly suit Freddy, who was very vain, but he had no option. Anyhow, far from putting him off, he belted it out louder and holier than ever. Obviously it made him feel good, hearing himself. He was a bag of nerves, but vain as a film star. Having a conversation with him was difficult—he couldn't seem to force his thoughts into words: his mouth opened and shut and nothing came out. Finish the phrase for him and he was liable to fly into a temper. Yet as soon as he burst into song the words poured freely, soared and stretched, he could do as he pleased—loop the loop if he wanted. That was why his narrow eyes flashed, his broad cheeks gleamed. He was exulting, victorious. His mouth yawned open, clean as a cat's. His voice rose out of his deep chest and bull neck, clear and pure, and he made it sob and quiver like an Italian's. You could almost see him listening to himself, congratulating himself on his eloquence.

He peddled dirty pictures—whether for money or not I wouldn't like to say. He could have passed them round for the kick it gave him, the feeling of power—there were blokes like that. It was funny in a grotesque sort of way, hearing him warbling away so angelic, pure as a nightingale, the next minute sliding the little top drawer of his toolbox in and out, hissing and spluttering as he passed out those grimy buff-coloured envelopes. He had a Hitler moustache, and his greasy reddish locks were impeccably combed and parted. He was a shiny, bristling, half-frightened and half-defiant rat. He sang well, but it was like listening to a medium, not really him. When he went off the deep end, fucking and blinding and his eyes rolling back in his head as if he was having a fit, his face turned white with fury and his head shook. It was a wonder his teeth didn't rattle, the way his rage boiled up in him. Other times he'd move jerkily like a puppet or a spastic. A real bag of nerves he was, like Pad, like Ginge, all of us. Except Bert Ferguson.

Bert was slow-witted, but not a fool. He was semi-skilled, which meant he was given the straightforward jobs, large batches of say a hundred at a time. All you had to do was set up your machine, go into a trance and keep ploughing away. He was happy to do that, the monotony was something he knew how to cope with. Interrupt him and he'd look at you bemused for a minute while he swam up to the surface. You could see him doing it. What he couldn't cope with was anything intricate and abstract; it baffled him, worried the life out of him and his genial spirits flagged. He kept going and fetching Pad, who confused him still further, unknowingly, his fingers as swift and intelligent as Bert's were slow and thick.

' Okay Bert?' he'd say, darting off to the next problem before Bert's head had finished wagging. Then I'd hear the poor bugger behind me with his head well down, concentrating, really trying hard and breathing heavy. I relied on Bert to keep me buoyed up; I only had to twist round and give him a grin for him to come out with his ' 'Ow are yer?' It was a way of saying fuck 'em all and what a war, what a life, *nil desperandum illegitimo carborundum* —don't let the bastards grind you down. A password. He had no ideas, Bert—it was the mere fact of him I seized on.

He was rocklike, sunny, he stood for something in my eyes. Gradually, over the year or two I worked with him, I built him up, romanticised him. Nobody else saw what I did, to the others he was only a happy bloke and a good mate to play darts with, drink a pint with: a bit thick. When he was made redundant, later, I gave in my notice as a protest and left as well. He got a job in mass production, on the track—over the road at Hammer Lane. I met him in a pub and he told me. I sat and supped the same draught beer he was drinking, that's how involved I was. Getting the sack hadn't worked him up as it had me, naturally. Outside we said all the best and went off in different directions. I never saw him again.

Another basically happy character, though with something leery underneath that would have been lost on Bert —who was wide-open, transparent—was Morgan over on the test bench. Taff they called him. Taking batches of finished work over there I made a beeline for him because he was the friendliest, the easiest to please. He rejected stuff here and there, he had to work to the limits on the drawing like everybody else or he was in trouble himself, but he let borderline cases through where his mates wouldn't, and if he had to chuck something out he'd do it apologetically. He was pleasant to deal with, and sometimes, to vary the scenery, I'd nip across to him for a quick chat, lounging against his table with the brown cork lino on top—the kind you get for doing lino-cuts at school. He was a checker, I was glad to have him for a pal; it was almost like being in with the bosses, only honourably. Until I saw he was no different from any of us. Worse, he was unproductive, and that gave him an inferiority complex. He was apologetic because he felt inferior. He sat on his arse in a clean white coat, passing judgement, and we were the ones, the producers, we were running him. It sank in slowly that these judges were on our backs. They acted like God Almighty, some of them, bluffed and blustered and it was an act, they were covering up. Attack was the best form of defence, they found. Taff, not being the belligerent type, licked his lips and said how sorry he was but you'd have to take it back and have another go. He was wary of the foreman and of wandering bosses from further afield—no end to them—and having a yarn he kept his fingers active most of the time, shifting cards and lumps of metal about on his table as if he was playing chess, keeping his eyes skinned, talking out of the side of his mouth. That was where he differed from Bert, who wouldn't give a bugger who was watching—if he wanted to talk, he talked. It wasn't a matter of defiance. The wormy fear and shiftiness wasn't in him, that's all. I idolised him for that, and it was a quality he was utterly unaware of. He hadn't a clue how rare it was. He thought everybody was the same as him. I had to be proud and tingling for him, on his behalf. I was a fraud, devoid of his unthinking fearlessness, it couldn't have been further from how I was then. This was another fascination and a bond. I set him up as a symbol, his rocklike quality, I charged him with meaning and gave him consciousness in my imagination. That was my role.

Taff was a dead loss in this sense of being material I could weave into a vision I was secretly working on, yet like Bert I'm sure he thought everybody was like him. In his case it meant being crafty, one jump ahead, and if you wanted a bit of life in the firm's time you had it on the sly. If Bert was guileless and clear, Taff was so naturally full of guile it was a kind of innocence. He was a trumpet player, a fan of Glenn Miller and Harry James. Our talks were mainly about music and instruments—I remember a conversation with him about the tone of the French horn—and I was beginning to hang my nose over trombones and trumpets in the record shops, seduced by Armstrong and Ory. If you have a valve instrument you need flexible joints to your fingers, he told me, and flexed his fingers to show me. He ran them up and down on the lino as if they had a life of their own. Another hobby of his was knitting, he said, and now he was watching me closely, allowing a little pause for me to laugh. ' Go on,' I said. Week-ends he'd knit pullovers and socks and God knows what, for enjoyment. He was small and rosy, married, with this sly side to him. The knitting was good finger exercise, too, he explained, and he gave me a nudge. ' Know any others?' he said.

His eyes slithered around while he chatted, for ever on the watch. This used to unnerve me. I didn't realise he had stuff from Freddy until one morning he slipped a buff envelope across the table. 'Have a look at these,' he mumbled, barely moving his lips. He touched his dago moustache with his fingertips and gave me a shiny grin and I knew then. I went speeding off to the shithouse with them: not the nearest, I had to have one with doors.

I felt I was heading for an interview with a prostitute, for the punishment cells, for a dose of self-inflicted, joyless pleasure. The envelope was in my back pocket—I could feel it crinkling as I walked—buttoned down tight for safety, and its power was flowing all over my body, stripping me before everybody. I got into an empty shithouse and perched on the seat without taking my pants down. Because the doors had no locks I sat with my right leg out stiff, using my toe as a wedge. The pictures waited, every second more urgent, they were ready to leap out on fire of their own accord. I fumbled and dragged them out, these greasy bits of card no bigger than playing cards, that could make you grovel. Black and white, pitiless, the players bollock-naked and nasty, their bodies lurid and starved of daylight. I bored into them, ravenous, shameful, I wanted to groan out loud. A woman sat on a chair, her legs apart and a man nuzzling at her, sucking her off. She'd got hold of another man's cock, he was squeezing one of her tits and her head was thrown back, her eyes closed and a drugged expression on her face, almost a look of pain. Hospitals, I thought of—an operation; it had that kind of surgical nakedness. One picture showed a cock in close-up, with this same woman guzzling thirstily at it, drooling, opening her mouth and lapping at the huge anonymous prickhead for all she was worth with her tongue. Others were orgies and the camera lens was defeated by arms like thighs, bellies and arses and black burrowing heads all entangled in a heap. My own cock was twitching about and I unbuttoned my flies and let it free and squeezed it, as the man was squeezing the woman's tit. That woman's drugged, suffering face tormented me for days, weeks after. I put the photos away and dropped them on Taff's table on the way back to the machine. He looked mean and shifty now, more than I'd noticed before. Everything looked meaner, the blokes bent and greyish, the old ones, and even the youngsters were sickly pale. More than anything else those pictures ripped me away from childhood, killed the magic and mystery. Now I had dead eyes, I was without hope, a man. I dropped the envelope on his table, he used the edge of his hand like a rake and scooped it straight into a drawer, out of sight.

'Any good?'

He flicked me a glance, idle, not concerned.

'Bloody hell,' I said, trying to sound merely impressed. He raised his head mildly, in hopes of a chat. I kept going. I could have killed him, innocuous as he was, for sitting there so immune after unleashing that lot. The same went for the source, Freddy. I was trapped once more, a year or two later, going by Freddy's machine, and he was flicking through a whole pack of cards for Ginge's benefit, who stood sniggering his appreciation. What he'd got hold of was a series of drawings based on the strip characters Dagwood and Blondie. There was Dagwood, his startled look, hair parted in the middle as if by a bullet, a couple of hairs poking straight up on the top of his head, and Blondie had her famous gormless expression. The difference was in their antics. There they were in suburbia, they'd be fucking away in various positions, mostly acrobatic, and the captions underneath were supposed to be funny ha ha. Nobody read them, they were too busy soaking up the pornography. In one sketch, Dagwood was spreadeagled on the carpet of the living-room, looking absolutely helpless and astounded, as if transfixed by the sight of his own prick. Blondie, her dress yanked up, stocking tops flashing, had impaled herself on it or was easing herself down with her back to him, her hands on his knobbly knees to steady herself, head lifted up, her eyes round and doll-like, and facing her the door was opening and her mother coming through it on a surprise visit, carrying an armful of parcels. 'Oh hello Mom,' it said underneath, 'how nice of you to drop in!'

I saw one or two over Ginge's shoulder, a sickly smirk on my face in case somebody was watching my reactions.

They were the power and the truth, the dynamo, the missing element. Callous and vicious, they jolted you with electric shocks, bit into you with their cutting edges, sudden as blows. Cut through the dolour, the torpid heartbreak—you twitched in your pants, sickeningly, nauseatingly alive. It was worse then, it put the burden on you to do something, fuck off, and the other way was a kind of sleep, a torpor. Either way it was a bundle of sensations, starting in the dark and ending in the dark. You sleepwalked. Rode through the back gate showing your identity card to the copper who wasn't looking, but you never knew for sure, he may have been peering through the slits of his pill-box. Lifted your bike into the racks, took off the pump and clumped in, and it was getting light in the slush of the sky, kindling a dingy brightness. In the main shop everything congealed and lifeless, the belting hung slack, yellow lights shone on the myriad surfaces, and with eyes still gummed with sleep you noticed things, the matt dryness of the belts, the dry light on the papers, tables, the stagnant milky scum on the suds, the gloss of light on the enamelled casings of some of the machines, the oily sheen of others, the glitter of cogs, the tapering points of drills, the brittle curls and loops of lathe cuttings jamming the innards, frozen billowing heaps, the black mounds of swarf. The early birds were in already, propped upright here and there, reading the papers and waiting for the first hooter. It was bleak as a cemetery till you reached the spot where you belonged, then the familiarity stirred in your chest like a vague comforting smoke. The first hooter yelled a warning and the final one at eight sounded harsh as an order, raucous. Pad bustled in with a minute to spare, hopping down the gangway on one foot, dragging off his cycle clips. His face still bleary, fingers straightening the mess of his collar he nipped up and down the line scratching at his head, digging at his arse, delivering his morning greetings and salutations.

' Fit, George?'
' I feel champion.'
' Bert?'
' 'Ow are yer?'
' Morning, Ken.'

126

'What's good about it?'

This was Ginge, but Pad couldn't stop for an answer, he was trotting back to the head of the column, cranking away madly at the top handle of his machine, about to let battle commence. He was the pace setter and exemplar. If he didn't kick off on time, none of us did. So he dug immediately at the green button, his machine whirred and hummed. He made a few preliminary adjustments, waggled the dust suction pipe a little lower, stuck the diamond tool on the flat laminations of his chuck and turned on the magnet. He twirled the diamond under the rim of his wheel and trimmed it. A cloud of grey dust rose up. Then he was away, working, the sparks flew in showers, in purring flickers for the finishing cuts. In a sudden agitated burst and flurry he dives for his fags, in the bottom drawer of his toolbox. Lights up, and while he draws it down and sighs gratefully, he seizes the opportunity to glance round at the rest of us. He might be admiring the view, his gaze is so vague and drifting and unfocused. A thought hits him, he grabs a work card and darts off through a gap in the machines to see a progress chaser.

It may have been Ted Hines he was seeing, or one of his mates. Ted infatuated me—he was another one I had no contact with, nothing direct, other than watching him strut past, cheeky, brash, with his irresistible charm and zest, his wide grin, broad shoulders and narrow hips, a little hollow in his back and his chest out, breasting along. He was zippy, eager, his good looks were the craggy, low-brow kind, he was the open-air type, ready to talk football any time, bubbling over to tell somebody about the blinder so-and-so played on Saturday, and his reactions were dazzlingly quick, he was seasoned just right with a touch of cynicism so that his high spirits had force, they were infectious even at a distance. He was out of my age group altogether, in his twenties, which was ideal for me. It made familiarity impossible, I could get an eyeful of him and he wasn't even aware of my existence. He zoomed up and down : once he caught me at it, our eyes met and he gave me a broad wink. But he hadn't a clue what my game was. He was all on the surface; that's what gave him brilliance, such a turn of speed. He had a mass of short black hair, tight energetic curls, boyish, and underneath this mop his pale face was tough and firm, like an intelligent, gentle boxer's, and like a boxer's it manifested the power of his body. I was able to transfer the tweed jacket and suedes from Chirpy Birdsall to him, for he wore the same sort of rig-out; only his jacket had patch pockets and a couple of pleats in the back. He swaggered, swung his shoulders like a sailor on leave, with the natural arrogance of the lithe young hopeful who knows his popularity. His quick grin and high-pitched croaking voice got a welcome in the most unlikely places. I saw real tetchy old bastards with their faces cracking in an attempt to raise a smile for him. Nothing tarnished his innate modesty. Down in the club-room under the canteen at dinnertimes I'd sit watching him in table tennis matches—he belonged to the team—and though he didn't dominate by any means, his vigorous, crisp returns and the habit he had of letting himself be forced back and back, crouching, fighting a defensive battle, captivated me more than if he'd been winning. He was my star. I got endless pleasure from watching his stance, his movements, hearing his yells of triumph, his fresh happy laugh. If you have a hero, he can do no wrong.

Most of the kids I was growing up with had the usual heroes which they were happy to share, on the screens, on the sports field. I had screen ones, like them, and stars of the concert platform like George Weldon who conducted the Birmingham Symphony at the Town Hall, a handsome limping figure ringed around by students on the hard cheap seats behind the timpani, high up like gulls on a cliff, clutching tight and earnest at their scores, as worshipful as fans at a pop concert. And they yearned over him, his white ravaged face, the forelock he kept flinging back impatiently, his wild tormented antics at the crescendos, writhing over the strings, the woodwind, dragging poetry by the scruff out of the leader, who sat impassive sawing away, bland as a businessman at a council meeting as George fought and suffered, raising the pitch of life, plumbing the depths of feeling—and then the moment, the sign, the message, flung arms of crucifixion as it killed him, the cost was so great. We died with him in consummation and it wrung our hearts, the glory, the greatness; a triumph of death. The sedge withered but we'd come right through and out the other side, George hung his head and we stormed applause at him, threw garland after garland, he was dead on his feet, swaying, absolutely shagged. For us, for us. And more heroes had been forged, we were linked now in a wonderful immediacy to the dreams of epoch-striding giants, Beethoven, Sibelius. George limped away, Byronic, stepped down from the cross, a flicker of a smile on his face. Tall and dark, lame—and we stumbled down the back stairs in a daze, wreathed in beauty and reconcili-ation, out to the harsh light, New Street, walking on the eggshells of dreams, shattered by the everyday, wan and attenuated and lost as lovers. That was what we loved him for—he took us with him, breaking the barrier, he fought through to the realm of fabulous, splintering light at the centre of each of us, our body and soul. He heaped riches on us, made us seven feet tall. The same thing happened in jazz, only more humorous, human, less grandiose, and we had to do it from the record or with the aid of local groups who had no aura, who were ordinary dull fellows acting as mediums.

I had these shared heroes like everybody else, and I had the secret, special ones, like Ted Hines. They belonged to me, nobody else, they were my creation. One thing they all had in common was that they were liberators. And the villains put you in chains. I was in chains from the begin-ning, almost from birth, because everything menaced me. Villains such as Chirpy Birdsall, petty sadists, shits, they had me in chains and I was craven, I had a craven desire to crawl, be fawning—I was like a dog that tucks in its arse and drags across the floor to lick the boot that ill-treats it. Then one day I found myself face to face with a villain who sickened me. I was shit-scared of him but the craven feeling had left me. I wanted to kick back, and I did. Where I found the guts I can't imagine; I marvel at it even today. Before him I'd had a dose of Flanagan, the grey-coated foreman with a foul temper and a mouthful of rotten teeth like rusty nails, who was in charge of the

I

engine fitters. I was on his section for six months, every day a misery. Coming up silently behind me he had the same paralysing effect as the teacher. He was a black Dickensian brow-beater, all black, exaggerated out of all proportion. 'You're doin' it wrong, aincha?' he'd ask with terrible soft politeness. Then the enraged bellow straight at your head, 'WRONG!' His roar carried to adjacent sections, heads of the curious lifted, eager for the spectacle of Flanagan stamping back to his bench, which had a sloping hinged lid. He stood with his belly pressed against it as if he was behind a lectern. He was famous for these raving, savage tantrums. I was craven before Flanagan, my loathing was reserved for the fatuous grins of the spectators, the prying eyes watching safely in anticipation. My despair soaked down to my feet, saturated me, when I had to approach him and ask for another job. He was never real to me, but a mythical fiend in a nightmare I'd wake up from one day. According to legend, he had his knife in one fitter to such an extent that the poor sod turned, in the midst of a bollocking, and let him have it, bash, right in the eye. It caught him off balance and Flanagan went sprawling. Of course the bloke got his cards. Next morning there was a brass plate screwed into the floor on the very spot, with the legend engraved on it, 'Fighting Flanagan fell here.' Everybody believed it, so perhaps it happened. It was the kind of fantasy which came alive in the very force and desperation of your desire.

17

I'm inching nearer to him, that jaundiced, kite-faced bastard of a works engineer who taught me self-respect. I ought to be grateful to him for that at least. I want to catch his full flavour, the noiseless contained prowl, his stiff scraggy neck, the head poised like a cobra's. The poison wasn't in his tongue, it came spitting out from his eyes. He had the bleak look of a killer, as if the heart had been cut out of him at birth. I was leaning against the bench one morning, either in a dream or having a breather, and like a fool I had my back to the main gangway. A finger jabbed into my ribs woke me up rudely. I swung round, startled, to find this blazing snake head confronting me. It was like a clout between the eyes. I couldn't think what he wanted, I still hadn't got the message—I thought he wanted to have a word with me about something, perhaps a transfer to another section.

' Get on with it,' he said, not raising his voice. ' We don't pay you for that.'

I turned away burning and picked up the file and started scraping away at the lump of cold steel in the vice. Up and down, up, down, in a turmoil, never raising my head, and all the time it sank into me with iron hooks and teeth, deeper and deeper, his message. I was selling my labour, the hours and days of my life, to this congealed bastard. So that's it, that's being a worker, that's what it means! I felt deeply, bitterly ashamed. I stored it up, hid it away like everything else shameful and went on outwardly the same. I looked dead, I *was* dead near enough, but inside me now there was a white flame licking round my guts, a secret rage. I didn't come up against snake head again for another year or two—I'd catch sight of him in the distance and instinctively lower my shoulders, get on with it. Then after the war, on the machine grinders we had a rush of work and the old cry of overtime went up. In wartime they had the perfect excuse, but now it was different. I got the impression that the whole section, except Pad, was sick of long hours. I was, and it was voluntary, and I'd reached the point where my leisure was the only thing that really mattered to me. Now it was being threatened. I amazed myself; I was ready to fight. They were getting at me where it hurt, that's why. And I was single, so they couldn't twist my arm there. Pad was coming down the line, after an interview with the foreman, trying to wheedle us into saying Yes all right. Nobody wanted to work over, but for some reason nobody would say so. ' I'll work if the others work,' Bert said, and so said George, so said Freddy. It was like a refrain. When he got to me with his ' How about you?' I gave him a flat no. And a strange thing happened. A terrific feeling of pride shot through me. I was a rebel—

I'd refused. Nobody had made me do it, I wasn't bending to fit the situation. For once I was actually in charge, calling the tune, standing up for my rights. I felt intoxicated with a sense of power, and it was a revelation, it went counter to my whole idea of myself. I never dreamt it was in me, this stubborn streak. Well, I knew I was stubborn, but Christ—out in the open and fighting? It was nuts, a kind of suicide for me; I had no punch, no defence, I was a skin short. It was asking for trouble, surely. The others were looking at me a bit startled and abashed, and there was even a hint of admiration. I liked it. My scalp tingled, my hands were sweating. I was the quietest of the whole bunch, no one had expected me to turn out an agitator. Pad scratched his head and said :

' You mean you won't even if the others do?'

' It's voluntary isn't it?'

' Oh yes—voluntary.'

' Well you've asked me and I've said no. I'm not volunteering.'

' I'll have to tell Mr Gutteridge, it's not my fault, don't think I'm running . . . he'll want to know so I've got no option . . .'

' That's fair enough.'

He went scurrying off and I stood there feeling heroic, conspicuous and quaky but still in charge of the situation. I waited for the next wave. The first round was mine. Fantastic how strong it made you when you knew exactly what you wanted and had made your mind up and, best of all, had nothing to lose. It was giving me pleasure because it was so foreign to my furtive nature, and my mates were all helpless, waiting for the next move. With the new threat to my free time I had an enemy, clear and visible, and I had the urge to fight. I glanced round at them almost pityingly, my mates, waiting speechless and gutless. All of them together were weaker than me. I couldn't get over it. Standing at the machine I made the motions of working, and inside I was on my toes dancing, weaving in and out, brilliant feints, ducking and dodging and throwing lightning punches. I'd drawn blood and I was eager for more. I think if that had been the end of the affair, a bloodless victory without another shot being fired, I'd have been badly disappointed.

I was expecting the foreman. Instead, a shop steward turned up—a bloke I hadn't set eyes on before. A tall, doleful, lantern-jawed character, with bloodshot eyes and a loose mouth. He pushed up close, matey and intimidating, and to my amazement started trying to talk me out of it. He realised I wasn't in the union—apprentices weren't allowed to join—and for that reason he advised me to quietly drop the whole business. As I wasn't a member, his union had their hands tied. If the management turned nasty and gave me the sack, what could the union do about it? They'd be helpless.

'I get you,' I said. 'Thanks anyway for the advice.'

'You'll work then?'

I shook my head. 'Sorry.'

'Well, look out,' he said, and gave me a sour look. 'I know what I'm talking about, mate.'

I stood there motionless, tight as a wound spring, smiling calmly, and heard myself say these astounding words:

'They can sack me if they like. I couldn't care less.'

The shop steward shrugged, obviously disgusted. He opened his hands at the same time in the gesture which meant, That's it, then, my son, if you will persist in your folly. He moved off a couple of feet and looked at me in silence, lugubriously, with the mein of a parson. I stared back with as steady a gaze as I could manage. Then he swung back, hand on my shoulder, talking into my ear in a lowered voice:

'As a matter of fact, it was the management that sent me round to have a talk with you. Listen mate, I'll be honest, there could be a lot of people involved in this. A hell of a lot. Get me? It ain't just you being pig-headed we're worried about—I don't give a bugger about that myself. D'you follow me, brother? So think it over, that's all I'm saying. Don't do anything rash till you've had a good think about it. I'm not saying you are, but you *could* be raising a precedent. It could make things very awkward for a lot of folks. Okay? Think about it, brother, that's all I'm asking.' He patted my shoulder, placatingly.

'Okay,' I said, anything to get rid of him. He gave me a big confidential wink and pushed off. I looked round quickly, and heads ducked down hastily. I was the king-pin, I couldn't back down now. A day went by, then another. Nobody said anything, but everybody was wait-ing, like me, to see what happened next.

Pad came darting up, pink and flustered. 'Will you go to the foreman's office please?' It gave me such pleasure, that 'please'. My workmates were watching slyly as I marched off feeling ridiculously exalted, like Joan of Arc going to meet her judges. I was shaking and shivering, but that was nerves, excitement, anticipation, not fear. My great moment had arrived. When I got to his glass pen I saw the works engineer standing up at one end, one hand stuck in his trouser pocket. He had a habit of jingling coins when he was really savage. I knocked on the door respect-fully and marched in, and that was what he was doing, old Snakehead, rattling away at coins or keys. He was glaring coldly out across the vista of machines and benches into the far distance, as if bored stiff. He didn't even acknowledge my presence. The foreman, Gutteridge, looking angry and agitated, rushed up and started on me without wasting a minute. I'd been asked to work overtime in a proper manner and I'd refused, what's more I was holding up the rest of the section, urgent work was jammed in the pipe-line, it was utterly stupid and disgusting, selfish, unco-opera-tive. He barged on, until at one point I managed to mur-mur:

'I'm sorry . . .'

He must have thought I was being funny, because he lost his temper completely and screamed: 'You're not, you're not sorry, not sorry at all! Don't tell me you're sorry!'

The works engineer decided to make a move. He strolled over, bored and contemptuous, with an off-hand attitude meant to convey that he wasn't acquainted with the facts of the case, he was only there by accident but let's see what he could do.

'Tell me this, sonny,' he drawled. I looked him full in the eye, quivering from head to foot, thinking. You shitbag,

I'll tell you all right in a minute. 'Say you were coming to work in the morning, and you saw a blind man who wanted to cross over the road. Would you rush straight past, or would you stop, thinking of someone other than yourself, and help him to cross over?'

I managed a tight little smile. He was on with the same game, smiling. It must have looked comical, us two, glimmering frostily at each other like a couple of death's heads.

'I'm afraid I don't get the connection,' I said.

'You don't? It's perfectly simple. Mr Gutteridge here is in a spot. He's asking you to help him out of his difficulty, that's all. Just that. Asking you to act unselfishly for once.'

I began to feel trapped. 'I thought it was voluntary.'

The hate came up behind his eyes then, the killer look.

'He's asking,' he said softly, 'just as that blind man on the edge of the pavement's asking.'

'That's hypothetical. I don't know any blind man, I'm sorry.'

He raised his eyebrows at the use of that big word. Abruptly he changed his tack, stopped playing about. 'You a Communist?'

'No.'

'Your father a Communist?'

I shook my head, still smiling, goading. The glory feeling had come back. The tension slackened. He was miles off now, and visibly rattled.

'Read Communist books?'

'I don't see it's anybody else's affair, what I read,' I said, and for the first time felt inflamed by a sense of real injustice. He was sneaking my glory away, giving it to the Communists. It's me, nobody else, I wanted to shout. Can't you see I'm here by myself? The pride of the artist burned up in my face. All my own work. What the hell was a Communist book anyway?

'You won't help us, then, is that it?' he was saying, and I guessed by the sneering tone it was all over, I was being dismissed.

'I'm sorry . . .' I said again, lamely, forgetting the effect this had just had on the foreman.

The works engineer had turned his back. He jingled his coins and played pocket billiards, staring out of the window again.

'All right,' Gutteridge said wearily. What an act. He wanted me to feel I'd stabbed him in the back. I went out politely, closing the door, fighting hard against the guilt they were wishing on me.

Still quivering from the conflict, I walked back to the square foot of factory floor where I stood all day, working and dreaming violently, the spot where I belonged, felt safe, even liked—except that now, more and more it was becoming irksome. One by one, they all asked me—Pad first, he was terribly anxious—'What happened?' He looked sick and worried as it dawned on him that nothing had really altered and the situation was unchanged. And when he came up to me next morning, first thing, wringing his hands and almost in tears, saying what a fix he'd be in at home if he couldn't work overtime any more, flat time just wasn't enough to meet his commitments, pay his hire purchase, his mortgage, shoes for the kids, he'd come to rely on his overtime and he couldn't work now if I didn't —begging me outright to say yes for his sake—I just nodded and said 'Okay then—one night a week and no more.' He was in a dreadful state, making a disgusting scene as he went to pieces in a desperate attempt to put on a convincing performance. His face lit up and he scurried off mumbling how grateful he was, and I felt stupid and flat, it was so pointless after all. Yet I'd won, hadn't I? Even that seemed in doubt. What else could I do, faced with that kind of grovelling desperation? I'd won, but this turn-about-face sucked the pride out of me, and it rankled for days, the thought that the bosses would believe they'd talked me round.

I kept thinking about the questions that shitbag had snapped out all of a sudden. Are you a Communist? Now I knew he was so sensitive on the subject, I began to look on his opponent the works convenor with real respect. They said he was a dedicated Communist, and I believed it. He was pint-sized, he worked one of the massive shuddering planers, it towered over him as he watched the huge table sliding back and forth, he'd tap the tool over another fraction of a turn and the cast iron would spray off the raw strapped-down casting in a rasping fountain of hot chips. His hands were permanently black from the iron dust and he'd be seen marching through the shop on his way to the offices like that, bow-legged and fearing nobody, a tough, charred, indomitable figure, a bit of black moustache over his lip as if the back of his hand had smudged it on.

Dinnertimes, in the summer, he'd have a group of apprentices squatting round him outside on the grass verge, his back against the railings of the Ferguson empire, giving anyone who'd listen a run-through on the history of the union movement. Derek Newey would be there with a bundle of *Workers* and a tin mug for a collection, smiling down his nose and bathing in reflected glory. I could never make out this strange allegiance, the cordial, elegant and rather wish-washy young man and Alec Jenkins, his middle-aged, furrowed face and gritty, bitten-off speech, his cold blue twinkling eyes, his bitter relish for the old class war. Derek was interested in the theatre, as distinct from bookish, which I was, and for a time I cultivated him. He dabbled and wavered, and it shook me, most pleasantly, to realise that he valued my opinions. It wasn't so flattering when I got the hang of him and understood that this cultivated young fellow with his cigarette holder and his urbane, cool manner, a man several years my senior, heard me out solemnly and seriously only because I had prejudices, likes and dislikes, when it came to books and writers. For some reason he found this remarkable. He had none of my intolerance, in fact he couldn't make up his mind about anything. He wobbled like a jelly. His Communist affiliation wasn't so incongruous either now I'd got to know him better. It was romantic flirting, with no risks attached. He sat cross-legged on the grass like a Gandhi disciple near the acrid little working-class realist and it was too daft for words, like Beauty and the Beast. It was coming up to the General Election and soon the Communist candidate arrived to deliver a roadside speech. Here was Alec Jenkins' equal, an army captain recently demobbed who'd emerged from the ranks during the war, a black-haired, hard-built young Scotsman, thick neck and craggy shoulders, roaring harsh and strong against the traffic, hammering home his points with his fists, one-two, the greatness of the Labour Movement, the exploiting bosses, the solidarity of the workers. Only a handful listened, the lorries drowned him and he fought harder, croaking like a raven, with Alec Jenkins crouching at his feet, unmoved, hard and fixed and invincible. And a fortnight later we were all out, the union had called a one-day token strike. I went down in the town and joined the mass meeting, on the platform the union leaders called for a show of hands, and a forest of arms shot up. I had no idea what the dispute was all about; it was no concern of mine. It was the show of strength and the solidarity which impressed me. A strike gave you an illusion of movement and power that was exciting; it was a flag of defiance hoisted in the very face of authority, telling you to stick together, unite. I shifted position in the crowd, working a little nearer, on my own, vaguely stirred by the restlessness and discontent, taking no notice of the speeches—which I couldn't hear properly anyway. I liked the atmosphere of it and I liked my anonymity, being merely a face in the crowd, feeling the ripples of unrest wash over me. Something was on the move, it felt good. Next day we were back at work, nothing had changed, we were all stuck, we all had our different reasons, excuses for being caught by the short hairs. We were caught, that's all I knew. My real escape routes were more and more to be found mapped out in books. Nothing could beat the excitement of finding in a book the thoughts and dreams and emotions, the frustrations, disappointments, achings that corresponded with yours, whispering and confiding and trusting you like a lover. That was what I was now, a book lover. I was beginning to live vicariously, to recognise myself as some sort of exile. At Lillington during the war I used to sit in the reference library of a Saturday afternoon, the light slowly turning purple outside the steamy high windows as I opened the big tomes, the potted biographies of modern authors. A writer was somebody else —even a modern one—and I was as curious to see their photos as I was to read their life stories. I'd stare avidly at

Joyce with his black eye patch, looking sickly and piratical. I remember the fascination of the queer word Proust, that I didn't know how to pronounce though it half rhymed with *sprouts* to look at, and took on vegetable properties because of the coincidence. I held it in my mind afterwards and juggled it, fingered and toyed with it; it was crisp, crunchy, with a touch of frost, or cooked soggy and water-logged, spiced back to life with a squirt of vinegar. A short story I read at this time, by a young American, was about a lonely Negro boy who, towards the end of the tale, sat at the kerb and cried softly, and *the tears splashed into the dust at his feet*. Softly. Reading that word, and the phrase about the tears, I was overwhelmed with longing to create feelings of desolation just as powerful for myself. It seemed terribly necessary and important. I didn't ask why, I just wanted to do it—make the world cry real heartrending tears as they read my words. The same thing happened when I read Saroyan's *Daring Young Man* story, only that took me further, I wanted the sense of desolation to sing and triumph in a crazy way. There was a broad avenue of chestnuts in Lillington, leading very firmly, with a slow dignified sweep, to the main road. Either side were select, big houses, each one trim and enclosed as a mansion in its own grounds. Weekdays I cycled between the trees in the dark if it was winter, swishing over the leaves if it was autumn, and in the summer on hot Sundays I'd walk half-way up the avenue and branch off to the left up a public path leading out to some meadowland. I read *Daring Young Man* out there, lying in a nest of long grass, feeling blue and melancholy and elongated, yet part of a gay com-position—like Chagall's poet. What a blood transfusion that story is, what doubt and confusion too, what debili-tating sadness. I gathered up the swirling dizziness, the truth, the meaning, I pitied everything and everybody, I saw what was in store for each one of us. ' Man that is born of woman has but a short time to live.' The blue sky emptied, it looked blank and threatening as it does at moments of crisis in childhood. I was seventeen. I got to my feet and stumbled off home hurriedly, and was glad to be clumping down the area steps into the basement, glad to be holed up, shut off, huddling together like any family of animals for warmth and comfort.

But I knew now. These were deep secrets, closely guarded. The whole world of books was liable to be blotted out by a word in those days, it had to be fenced round protectively against the doctrine of common-sense I lived with, the material, practical routine acknowledged as real. Derek Newey's lack of awareness irritated me no end. Surely it was plain enough, the hostility of the treadmill to anything as useless as art? No, blithe as a curate he'd wander over to my side of the factory to ask my opinion of Huxley, say, or Wells or Shaw, his butterfly mind flitting to and fro delightfully. I'd handle him very warily. I much preferred to go over to his section and talk to him, I wasn't so ashamed of him over there. It was incongruous talking to him at any time, anywhere, nutty, especially in that place of formidable industry, grinding and bashing and screwing, making, churning it out—but it was no use mentioning that to him. Anyway it was all right listening to his moonshine, it made a change. I felt safe enough where nobody knew me. That was how I met Vincent, a fitter in his thirties, fair, with a big wet mouth and dirty teeth. He'd heard us talking and one day he chipped in with—' I've done a spot of the old writing meself, you know—excuse me for butting in, I'm an ignorant bastard aren't I—go on, say yes!' It seemed he wrote stories as a hobby, and he hinted that he'd had some of them published in magazines like *Argosy*. So from then on, if I was coming away from Derek's bench this Vincent at the far end would invariably collar me. He was a Dostoevskian character, he squirmed and twisted with inner contradictions and he had to expose them, humiliate himself. He oscillated between a humble-pie, Uriah Heep manner, so obviously phoney it made you blush, and a crude natural boastfulness he tried to tone down, knowing how unpopular it made him.

' Vince the bullshitter, that's me,' he'd say, breathing his rotten breath into your face. ' Now listen, don't take any notice of me, what I say. Lies, all lies. Bullshit. Ask anybody, they'll tell you. Pay no attention to Vince, they'll say. Ask Derek . . .' This was how he rounded off his accounts, or a piece of advice he was handing out gratuitously. Then he'd laugh violently, so forced it was even more offensive, suddenly switch it off and say, sotto voice, ' No, but seriously . . .'

At the very beginning I wanted to write stories rich with comedy, and the first story I ever wrote was based on Vincent. It was supposed to be funny. The elaborate, creaking humour and bombastic vocabulary, the excessively dignified style, these were lifted straight out of *Oliver Twist*, a book that had made me laugh out loud on one page and brought me close to tears the next. My story was a pen portrait of an obstreperous character who talked rapidly like Vince, who laughed like a horse, curling his lips back and baring his long stained fangs, head rearing, letting rip a mirthless whinnying sound. Vincent the Bullshitter I should have called it, but the word wasn't in Dickens' vocabulary —and that was where I came unstuck. Vincent was Vincent. He demanded his own language if he was going to live at all, and it had to be copious, flowing, spittle forming at the corners in tiny bubbles and bursting. I used to watch the bubbles and lose track of what he was saying. He was Vincent, nobody quite like him before or since, a unique pain in the neck—not Uriah crossed with Lebedev, add a pinch of Fagin and stir slowly. It was the other way round —he was the real thing, raw material, inspiration, and characters in books the pale reflection. He was a Cockney in the Midlands, he came from the hub of the world, the Smoke, and that made him more overweening than ever in this one-eyed town, and more uneasy, and squirmy, tying himself in knots with anxiety as he tried to be ever so 'umble. His gift of the gab earned him nothing but winks and knowing glances, distrust rather than derision. He was tolerated and that's about all. Instead of drying up in the face of this silent disapproval, the gab came out slimy and unctuous. It had to have an outlet, that was his trouble. He grabbed me as a likely ear, an audience. His mouth bubbled at the corners, his eyes slid from side to side : ' They're watching me, look—they think I'm delivering another load of bullshit !'

18

IT'S amazing the mates you pick up when you're passive and drifting, offer no resistance, smile meekly, show no preferences one way or the other. I find it terribly hard to say no to anybody; always have done. If I'd said no, can't stop, and kept walking, Vincent would have been left with his mouth hanging open. With other people it's not so simple. Tony Maggs, for instance. Tony was an apprentice I'd hardly nodded to indoors. Then on the push homewards at night, as the light evenings arrived, he'd ride up alongside me and we'd be shoulder to shoulder, pedalling mechanically, having one of those asinine conversations he specialised in. His yellowish turnip mush would suddenly slide into view, his thick lips splitting open in a grin of complicity, as if we shared a secret joke. At first I thought he was taking the piss, but no, it was his queer manner. He really liked me, for some cockeyed reason of his own he thought me funny—he actually enjoyed my company. This was flattering, and entirely unexpected, so, of course, I saw him in a new light and even got a kick out of him for a while, thick as he was. He had a sense of humour, I'll say that for him. On our first night out together—we went into town for a game of billiards and a drink—he told me something he hadn't told anybody before. ' In confidence, mind,' he warned me, and in fact he couldn't figure out himself why he wanted to tell me, of all people. Funny, it was. I was the kind of bloke who listened quietly without spoiling the yarn, he said, and another thing, he knew I didn't blab it around.

' Blab what?'

' What I'm going to tell you.'

' Oh.'

' Am I right or not?' he asked cagily, grinning from ear to ear.

' Go on, for Christ's sake,' I kept saying. ' Tell me the bloody story—stop beating about the bush.'

He chortled and nearly doubled up. In his simple-minded way he thought he was tantalising me, a big tease. I was bored to death already, itching for an excuse to cut the evening short. We were chalking the cues, the top half of the smoky upstairs room in deep shadow above the wide lights hung low over the table, bathing the emerald green cloth. A couple of players at another table under the big clock were talking in subdued voices. Down in the street a car buzzed by. I screwed down the hard lump of hollowed chalk on the tip of the cue. The dry scraping sound went with the stale air, the lifeless quiet, the feeling of deliberated movements and suspended time. Tony's confidential act had got the better of him now, he was up close with his face hovering around my ear. I made a feeble crack, sick of the whole performance. It made no difference what I said, he'd insist on reading something comical into it. Was I a comic and didn't know it? This thought excited me, it was a gift worth cultivating. I was still putting on the act of listening interestedly to Tony, a stupid grin stretched over my clock, but my mind was wandering. Then it happened, he was really telling me, urgent, his voice changed. The story hinged on the fact that his parents had gone out to Australia for a couple of years apparently—his old man was a compositor, who thought he'd go out on the ten quid assisted passage scheme, stay there the minimum and earn big money on the *Bulletin*, then work his way home and see the world at the same time. Tony's mother had a sister out there. I knew this was right anyhow because I'd noticed Tony flashing his mail around and shouting the odds. ' I got a letter from Alice Springs,' I heard him shout, ' I got a postcard from Bondi Beach ' or some such place. He had to find digs while his parents were away, that was the point. His landlady, according to his description, was a big flabby shag-nasty old cow, old enough to be his mother, who liked to take in lodgers so that she could always be sure of a bit. What was up with her husband? I wanted to know. Don't ask me, Tony said—he was a little runt, and if he argued the toss she'd drag him down on the carpet in front of us, stand over him like Britannia and tell him to admit defeat and shut his row. Charming set-up. Desperate and hopeful, she was, a slovenly old slut wandering round half undressed till dinnertime, piling up the dirty crocks in the sink for her husband to wash when he came in from the office at night, rattish and beaten, full of suppressed venom. A Devon woman. Now we were getting it, he was half breathing down my neck to tell me the rest of it. It seems he was on his way out one morning, going past the hallstand in the passage and out came Mrs from the middle room, slopping about in bedroom slippers and dressing-gown as usual, carrying a fresh towel. The next minute she'd blundered into him as if by accident and was pawing at him, saying he was only short but so hairy that it was plain he was a man already, and was it true what they said about short men being well endowed? In a flash she noticed the bulge in his pants. 'Oh my!' she was gasping, delirious at the very thought of it. 'Oh can I see it? Oh my, what a whopper—can I get it out?' Her loose cheeks were flopping, red with excitement, hairpins working free, she unbuttoned his flies and fished it out before he knew what had happened. 'Oh God, I wonder if I can touch it!' she moaned, frantic, throwing her towel over it, glancing round madly in guilt and panic and confusion. All Tony did was stand there pushed against the wall with his cock jabbing the air, rigid as a coat hanger. She kept whipping the towel over it, lifting the corner to have another look, to make sure it hadn't got away, gasping and spluttering in adoration, till in seconds he went off with an almighty bang. His spunk shot out with such force it splashed the front door, and the landlady was down on her knees mopping at the mess with her towel—almost with her nose in it, she was so short-sighted. It looked as if she was trying to lick it off, working away with her tongue out, and she was so delighted, grateful, apologetic, babbling away to herself. 'And then—fucking arseholes!—the doorbell rang. Christ, she nearly jumped out of her skin. "Just a minute, just a minute," she was yelling, scrambling up on her feet again, still mopping away for dear life.'

When I thought it all over afterwards, it rang true except for that last bit of crude embroidery—the doorbell. Even that was possible, I suppose, but I couldn't swallow it somehow, it was too easy to add on, and an irresistible touch for someone like Tony, who had to have it laid on with a trowel. I was living it till he got to that bit. I heard him tell the whole story again later to somebody else, and ' Fucking arseholes!' he ended, exactly the same, to convey his wonder and amazement.

I think of him, and then for pure contrast think of Peter Greenstreet. What deadened and stupefied when you were with Tony for any length of time was his lack of interest in anything that didn't have a horse laugh in it somewhere. The factory was all right, the town was all right, the flicks, life—what else was there? He was content, dead as a door-nail, and that damned him for me. How could anybody be so thick, such a simpleton? And I think more than any-thing, the one thing that got me about Peter Greenstreet—who had a very different, very enviable contentment—was his cleanliness. It was a most repulsive cleanliness that he possessed, the next-to-Godliness kind. The kind that accuses in spite of itself. He was good and kind and considerate, he was responsive, his sincerity shone out of him, he was naked in the world—like a flatfish on a fishmonger's slab. Nobody could question his utter integrity, he was worth a dozen Tonys, yet I couldn't raise a laugh in him or him in me. All I could ever do in his company was smile a watery forgiving smile at the world. No room for hate, no outlet, no chance to smash anything. After I left school I lost touch with him, then years later I bumped into him in town on a Saturday, and he seemed unchanged. If any-thing he was even more understanding, admirable, self-effacing. He suggested that we got acquainted again, re-newed the friendship. Once again I was trapped by my inability to refuse anybody; the word No froze on my lips. I agreed to go out to his place. Leaving him I started to seethe, to call myself names for making such an idiotic ar-rangement. I was twenty-one, beginning to smash out—it was either that or die. I got home and rushed upstairs to the box-room, shut myself in and wrote him a letter saying I'd given his suggestion a lot of thought but it would be useless, a waste of time—I was an atheist now. What I looked forward to was the end of organised Christianity, churches closing down for lack of congregations, the cathe-.

drals turned into museums and art galleries. I wrote this in a cold ruthless style, explaining that this wasn't so much an opinion as a self-evident process already under way. I'd been reading Shaw's *Prefaces* and I aped his calculated impertinence—it suited me to a tee. My maudlin anarchy and inner screaming threw me into incoherence. Smash, smash, that was all I could hear. This Shavian focus held in front of me was exactly right, I was able to write a letter that sounded unanswerable to me, a superb piece of logic-chopping, a cutting, devastating, inspired diagnosis, cool as a surgeon. The bit about atheism I put in to flatten him completely—it was the first time I'd used the word—and the rest was a series of body-blows aimed at his most vital parts, just in case he got up again. I finished like a real prig, telling him how futile it would be if we became friends again, we were opposed on every fundamental issue and there seemed no point in us meeting. What it was, I was afraid of meeting him. I wanted us to be opposed, enemies. Face to face he would gently listen, gently understand, gently but firmly take me by the hand and endeavour to lead me back into the fold. ' The place for criticism is inside the church,' he always told me. ' We need people like you to change things.'

Peter Greenstreet—to recall him in detail, at his most characteristic, means going through those Sunday rituals all over again. Nip upstairs straight after dinner, after washing my neck and ears in the back kitchen, bending over the yellow glazed trough with its chipped enamel bowl—brick walls still streaming with moisture, the condensed steam of that Sunday morning roast—and smelling the cabbage water, peering over the net into the yard of blue serrated bricks laid in a herring-bone pattern, on which a soft drizzle is falling. Upstairs I go to the bow-fronted chest of drawers and fetch out a clean white shirt as ordered, clean vest and underpants, laying them carefully on the bed by the side of my charcoal grey suit and waistcoat which is there already; searching intently for collar studs, cuff links, coming down transformed, feeling the stiffness of the starched shirt across my shoulders, the heavy cloth of the jacket weighing on my arms importantly; bending my knees self-consciously as I walk, with an unpleasant awareness of the strange elegance of my wrists. Marching into the kitchen with a hollow in my back to clean my shoes.

Peter Greenstreet was Sunday afternoon incarnate. The roseate glow of his cheeks, his pink lips a little too long and thin to be cherubic, his pink tongue, the pink insides of his mouth, his pink hands and scrubbed nails, pink as washed shells, his chubby knees, round and pink like fresh apples— he was the personification of the sweet soapy Christianity we were taught in that Baptist Sunday School. He sat beside me and became my friend, we were in the same class, grouped around our teacher in a halo of quiet in the dingy bare room behind the chapel, pushing back our hard chairs gingerly to avoid rupturing the sanctity. Sitting next to me with his elbows pinched in, his lips pursed, his gleaming black shoes tucked well back, exuding a mixture of prim rosy goodness and determination—I looked on him more as an example than an equal. I wasn't on his level of excellence and never would be. Having him for a friend was belittling. We were boys of the same age, but when it came to religion he had the finesse of a professional. His teeth were fiercely clenched on the good life, as if he'd been born to it. It was partly his upbringing, I found out later. He was without any swank or side, no airs about him at all, even though his father was a teacher. It wasn't Peter's fault that he was superior—he just was. When we were told to turn to a particular passage in the Bible, he had his open at the exact place in a flash. Old or New Testament, it was all the same to him—he was at home there as he was in his own back garden. Noticing me struggling, hopelessly lost, he leaned over discreetly and whispered the page number. Then he'd cough into his hand, take a spotless white handkerchief from the top pocket of his jacket and wipe his lips. Putting the handkerchief back he rearranged it as before, folding it along the ironed creases and tucking it away so that only a triangle showed. He had his own Bible, his own hymn book, his eyeballs shone with his own special brand of beatitude. Asked to read aloud, he positively sparkled. He sat forward tense as an alarm clock about to go off, and I remember what a surprise it was the first time

I heard him, when that thin reedy voice trembled out. He was nervous, and I couldn't get over that. Not *him*.

Mention his name and it swirls back, all of it—the constriction of that best suit, a first pair of long trousers, mooning up dead and blind Whatford Street on a Sabbath, stiff and correct as if on the way to a violin lesson, peering under the arch up the cobbled lane leading to a yard where they sold ice, great salty blocks, at the rear of Pemba Street. Walking correctly and feeling like a penguin, a little before 3 p.m., up the hill through the canyon of Whatford Street overhung by the Humber cliff—raincoat folded and hung over the forearm, trouser bottoms swishing, burnishing my shoes; getting nearer, feeling a kind of stagefright. On Easter Monday assembling in the morning at the market for the parade: each church, Sunday school, scout troop a separate contingent with its own banner— those huge flapping banners held aloft between two poles, with tasselled cords for guy ropes, and the men carrying the banners had leather holsters for the pole butts slung round their necks on broad straps: the bugles and kettle drums, parade marshals, police, first-aid, the proud banners emblazoned with the name of your chapel—and as we moved off the poles lurched dangerously and I held my breath. Coming back for the morning service after that tour through the streets was tame and yet good, I liked sitting cramped in the pews and kneeling on the worn hassock with my face still tingling from the cold wind on the hills, the corners, feeling the restlessness and excitement churned up by the parade all round me, the flushed cheeks, bright eyes. The service was always perfunctory, they gave you a bun and an orange and you went winging home, a swallow-dive of joy, downhill, heading straight for the fairground on Hyson Road.

Even as a boy I was conscious of what we were doing in those processions. We assembled beneath our own flags and then marched out under the windy, wintry sky, the high winds and flurries of rain, and the sky seemed to billow and unfurl over us like the banner of Christ. The men carrying the poles braced themselves as the banners filled like sails and tugged powerfully: it was right and proper,

nature had to be fought down, the indifferent streets waited
sullenly as we swung round corners, bugles blazing, pene-
trating one district after another, soldiers of Christ on the
march, child crusaders. It was a tableau, a symbolic act, but
it wasn't a game. Stirring, exciting, but you weren't supposed to be enjoying it. The sweet shops, stationery shops,
junk shops, cycle shops, factories, barbers, warehouses,
chemists, picture houses, baths, markets, chip shops we
passed were all closed—but by dinnertime the fair would
be open at the end of our street, spinning and blaring loud
and strong. Walking behind the banners I'd be all warm
inside imagining the fair, picturing it so vividly that instead
of my feet treading on macadam and tramlines they'd be
crunching over the cinders flung down between the stalls.
The thrill of a fairground was in sensations like that, wild
anticipations—and the real surging excitement was generated with the electricity they made themselves—if you followed the rubber leads running from stall to stall where the
light bulbs dangled in glaring rows you could track down
the sources of power and light; massive traction engines,
wheels wedged, flywheels spinning, canopies shuddering.
On the road these engines pulled loaded wagons in a close
convoy like a train; now they stood half hidden at the
far corners of the waste ground, stowed away behind the
sideshows, harmless giants, tethered like elephants among
the showmen's luxury vans. No, now I think of it, the
Easter procession wouldn't have been half as enjoyable if
the fair hadn't been there at the end like a glittering
promise. It was the light at the end of the tunnel. Otherwise it would have been grim and drab and purposeful, grim
as those marches through the November streets on Remem-
brance Sunday. The one procession that was wholehearted
pleasure, fun and frolic from start to finish was the summer
carnival. There was a touch of civic pride as the floats
swung into view, the lorries and brewers' drays and mag-
nificent carthorses decked with flowers and coloured
streamers, we cheered at each new burst of glory, the trades
and industries all represented, unions, ambulance, fire brigade, nurses, police, a festival staged for fun and blossom-
ing like a garden out of all the elements of a city, kaleido-

scopic, a winding medley of noise and colour. What made it so intoxicating, so infectious was the craziness, the careless rapture, the way the crowds lining the route participated, yelling encouragement, cheering and laughing at the clowns on pushbikes and stilts careering down the gutters, raking the air with their collecting boxes and tins, shaking them madly like castanets. Cheery old men with nutcracker faces were giving the thumbs-up sign from the lorries, doing crazy antics dressed in pyjamas, every kind of fancy dress, and by the time the leading lorries reached us they'd have the judges' award cards proudly displayed, 1st, 2nd, 3rd, sailing past in order of supremacy. The whole thing emptied into the vast green space of Albert Park and drained away, petering out naturally, and you followed it in and forgot it almost at once because of so much else going on: car raffles, ox-roasting, gas-filled balloons taking off mysteriously into the blue with a label attached, bearing your name and address; refreshment tents, treasure hunt, bands, a play park full of sand, a tent where lost children waited for their mothers—and you stared in at the waifs and strays behind the trestle table, at their tearstained faces, examined them curiously, big enough now not to worry, then suddenly uneasy and small in that rowdy vastness, people milling everywhere, and you went darting back to where you knew your parents were sitting placidly on spread raincoats on the grass. No rain for a month but the raincoats still had to go down, my mother pressed the flat of her hand on the turf and maintained she could feel the damp—maybe the dew had been heavy that morning, she said. We hung about, eating sandwiches and drinking pop, the adults kept unscrewing the flask of tea, and when it got dark we'd move over behind the pavilion for the grand finale, a giant fireworks display. We waited patiently for hours and it was never worth it, somehow it always disappointed, perhaps because we'd been waiting too long, expecting too much. Next year we'd wait again on the same grassy bank, a vantage point, slowly getting chilled, telling each other it won't be long now. Nobody remembered how lousy it was last time. We sat listening to the breeze rustling the grasses and leaves, watching the elms blacken as the light faded, letting the dusk sadden us inexplicably. We shivered our shoulders, felt a touch of cramp in our legs from sitting too long, and began to feel deserted, last-out, everyone drifting inwards to the snug lit homes. Everyone but us. Long before the fireworks finished, we were ready to go.

19

STAND at the bay window and peer down the road: Ray's coming. He's not in sight but he's coming. It's his night. Lift the trombone out of its coffin—tubes green with verdigris at the joints. Secondhand. Try not to think of someone else's slime and slobber. All I can play is 'I Dreamt That I Dwelt in Marble Halls'. Just to sound a full ripe note, sustain it long enough to work the slide in and out, is an achievement, a good enough satisfaction. My mother pokes her head into the room to tell me it's awful, like a dying cow. That's her joke. I keep blowing.

'No more, you'll strain something,' she says anxiously, seeing my veins stand out. I stop, lower the instrument, gulp, fill my lungs with air and blow again. No good. Dismantle it, shake out the slobber, reassemble it. Can't play it but I can dream. Kid Ory in marble halls. The garden gate clicks—I wait breathless for the knock. Nothing. Is he coming or not? In looks my mother again: 'Is he coming tonight?' He'll come, he's bound to come, this front room pulls like a magnet. Shelves in the alcove full of my books, a stack of records in the corner by the radiogram, including nearly a dozen yellow-label Deccas—Beethoven's *Missa Solemnis*. Walked in the music shop last Saturday morning, flush after pay day, and asked if it was in stock. Right, I'll have it, thanks very much—just like that. Why not? What else is money for? We played it backwards by accident the first time. Wonderful. As good that way as any other when you're in love. Instead of God, it's Beethoven. Beethoven is Love. Waiting, I am waiting. Sit at the piano as if I'm composing. I am composing. I pick out notes, sad, lonely, tender, more beautiful to me than the masters. I can't play the piano either. So what? The beauty reverberates under my fingers, a secret language. My mother's head pops in through the doorway again—'Hasn't he come yet?'

He'll come, he's got to. I'm playing his music on the piano. For him. I wait pent-up like a lover. *Black, Brown and Beige Suite* ready on the turntable—he hasn't heard it yet. When he does he loathes it, can't bear to listen and I have to switch it off. It's his mood, not Ellington. All day he's been submerged in this nameless black misery . . . but never mind. At first everything's fine. Dusk of a Saturday night in July, mild lapping breeze, so quiet and peaceful. I can't sit still. I can hear the blue grass of the carpet growing. In he comes, shining, smiling. 'How's the idiot?' he says, grinning his head off, with a touch of malicious amusement mixed into his normal humour. I'm perfectly attuned to him, so it's not lost on me, this warning tremor. 'So he feels perverse tonight!' I tell myself, and I might be thinking, What a beautiful night. Slow brown Sunday tomorrow. I am happy. The idiot bit refers to the Dostoevsky I'm wading through, not me. If I can think of a funny answer I'll give it, but anything crude or unseemly would be unthinkable. We treat each other tenderly, gently, we are attentive, endlessly sympathetic. This is the honeymoon of our friendship. The ambience is undoubtedly romantic, the emotional charge high up in the chest, spiritual. 'What was that you were playing on the piano?' he asks.

'Oh, just something I made up . . .' He nods, leans forward receptively, eager to discover riches in me, so of course I play it again; a lame, halting, meagre little tune, plaintive, and each note transforms itself in the air and becomes radiant. I fashion jewels in the air. My friend sits struggling to contain a black mood, sunk back in the armchair. Soon he'll unleash his perversity, when the record goes on, and I can't help him or help myself. His very presence enhances me, changes my flow mysteriously. I am languid, heavy-lidded. I love the world, love everybody, smiling at nothing like a maniac.

I remember how the first time I went round to his place in East Street I heard delirious music coming out of a house a few doors down from him, it was boogie-woogie piano and through the net I could dimly make out this bushy-haired figure with his back to the window cascading notes like a prodigal. 'That's Adrian Levis,' Ray told me. 'He's self-taught. You should hear him play a Beethoven sonata. I used to go around with him a lot but he's engaged now. We even wrote songs once, tried to—him the music and me the lyrics. They're a big family but nobody else is gifted like him. His old man's tone deaf and his mother can't read or write.'

Mostly it would be the two of us in Ray's front room, but once or twice I was with my brother Alan who had first met Ray and brought him round. We played records, and talked books, while Alan sat there in his amazing imprisoned silence. Was he bored? Once I found a poem he'd written in celebration of a jazz player—'Blues for a clarinetist'—nothing ever more. We sat and listened, cranked up the clockwork gramophone and ate the bread-and-butter tea his mother served up if it was a Sunday—sometimes with jelly and custard, cakes and hot sweet tea. Ray would nip out with a jug to the off-licence later to get draught beer for his father. This goes on steady as a pendulum, these visits, and then he is called up for his National Service, Alan drops away and we continue by letter almost without a break in the conversation. Nothing stops us now.

I am sending long letters to Ray at Portsmouth and shorter, parry-and-thrust affairs to a married woman in the north who owns a copy of *A Season in Hell*. She reads books, writes poetry, paints pictures—I can't get over it. My letters are deliberate and brilliant compositions, failures every one—nobody suspects. I deceive as easily as I breathe, everyone but myself. I try out different styles, act parts. I'm vigorous, healthy, life-giving in my letters to Ray, strong and steady as a rock, all my vagaries suppressed. No melancholia—the words bound off the end of the nib, caustic, buoyant, no connection with me. I inspire myself, read them through and feel genuinely uplifted. It's when the reply comes and I see how successful I've been that I'm uneasy. It becomes a source of embarrassment, after the elation dies away. In the ones to the woman I am much happier, devoid of morals—what does the truth matter? I take to it like a duck to water, the male-versus-female game. I thrash about in the most calculated and provocative attitudes, I make angry, passionate, labial noises. The limits are unmarked yet I am aware of them instinctively. Within these limits I know I can do what I like. I am out to fascinate, stimulate, attract, mystify. The letters are battles masquerading as poems. Sometimes I enclose verses—they are softeners, oblique flatterers. I cultivate a cunning innocence. At one point she even asks if I'm a Negro.

On a sudden impulse I have sent out stories to a magazine. The editor returns them one by one, rejection slips underneath the paperclip, with pithy comments scribbled on them which I cherish and soon have by heart. 'Read Thomas Wolfe and learn how to temper your bitter realism with philosophy.' I can't write anything nowadays but letters. They make contact at first blow, there's no intermediary—you work direct in human materials. I'm restless, I can't stay in at night. Rake through the local paper for likely films in any district. The night-time transforms the drab streets into a luxurious solitude which ululates and parts and whispers. I slip into it each time with a sigh. Walk down under the hideous new sodium lights, the pavement falling away softly, narcotically under my feet in the dark, cross over the deserted Birmingham Road, turn up a lane of black ashes and earth trodden hard as concrete. On one side a ragged hedge of privet, allotment railings, patched wooden gates, huge gunmetal padlocks with brass flaps covering the keyholes, on the other side the steel wire and stanchions of a factory fence, buttressed and barbed. In a warm numbness now I'm on my way to see Henry Fonda at the Carlton, round the corner from the Albion Belt Works. A tightness under my heart scares me—if I breathe deeply it stabs. Coming home in a daze through the same ghostly lane I find myself reliving the marvellous Fonda walk, his grief and helplessness, submission, dignity, all manifested step by step and not a word spoken. I get home and the house is in darkness. There is a strange atmosphere of stealth—they've gone to bed but are they lying awake up there listening? The little stabs of pain begin again. I must live, make haste and live . . . I sit at the kitchen table and write a letter to the woman in the north who has everything—home, husband, children—telling her I'm in love with her. I write it powerfully, like Fonda crossing a room. Same stance, same tone, same dog-like irresistible tenderness enlivened by conscience—I can hit it perfectly, the exact note, because it resounds in me, shakes me like a reed. Like an actor fully into his part I am absolutely convinced that this is the truth and I'm not aping anybody when I write ' I'm in love with you '. I am hopelessly in need of the attentions of this mature woman. I have her photo, know her interests, read avidly between the lines—a thrilled exclamation tells me I'm winning the battle of letters : strike now. Back rushes a reply— ' Don't ever write that again!' Victory is mine : we make a date to meet.

I step off a bus outside the market, in a city I've visited only once before, as an apprentice on holiday. There facing me at the bottom of the sloping cobbles, plastered over a high brick wall, are the black letters of a poster—I AM COME THAT YE MAY HAVE LIFE, AND MAY HAVE IT MORE ABUNDANTLY.

I wake up from a dream so powerful it pins me to the bed, I am overcome by its truth and simplicity. In the dream I picked up a newspaper and saw my picture, a review of my book and the writer's first words were all I needed to read :
' He is empty.'
I lie in bed wide awake trying to burrow back into the dream which is so terribly important to me, lying still in the warm sack of the sheets and letting its memory linger. It is still more powerful than my waking life. Before it fades I do recreate enough of it to decipher the full sentence which says ' He is empty as a whore '. I am full of gratitude to the man, whoever he is, for such understanding. I am empty as a whore who can't get stuffed. An old bag in Market Street with broken carpet slippers and a caved-in nose couldn't be emptier than me. I know books are nothing. I know everybody's lying, I know it's so much

straw, stuffing, I want to smash the radio, run into the street and scream 'Liars'. Defy the desolation. Find love. I prowl up and down longing to be stuffed. I take nobody's word, I believe nobody, trust nothing. If there was a God I'd say thank God for making life so empty and wonderful. When I was twenty-one I had a shattering dream of love. A very beautiful young woman had found me, gathered me up in her arms, I wept and laughed into her long hair as if taking refuge, we were overjoyed at finding each other, we recognised each other at once, I kept laughing and crying, blissfully happy and grateful, luminous with this great happiness, and when I woke up it was like a shipwreck, heartbreaking, I'd lost her for ever. Goodbye! And could have wept bitter scalding tears, but nothing would come. The dream choked me. It was a blend of ineffable joy and terrible desolation, that dream—as if I knew that time was running out and any minute I'd wake up and lose everything. Paradise lost—the anguish of the fallen angel. Nothing was said, not a word. A silent one-reeler, poignant as Charlie biting his nails in close-up at the end of *City Lights*. The Dream. I wrote it down exactly as I remembered—the first piece of writing that deeply mattered to me. A dythyrambic ecstasy. I was naked, stripped, how could I possibly show it to anybody? It's always been that way, the longing for protective colour and the impulse to strip myself naked—*let them see me as I really am*. Two desires that go on flatly contradicting each other and conflicting—the involuntary shrinking back and the reckless demand for intimacy at any price, culminating in the worst ordeal, the final disgrace of humiliation by public exposure.

And quietly, slowly, in an entirely English, unassertive, decent sort of way I was going nuts in that place. That factory, that home, that town. I had to get out. I'd see Ray at week-ends, we'd shoot off on bikes, and two or three evenings a week we sat in the front room, ours or his, never mentioning it directly, our burning predicament, but primed with books and paintings, great men, great music, primed with the future and plotting for the new life to come like revolutionaries. We'd go on sudden unplanned holidays to Wales, the Hebrides, using the Youth Hostels, and now and then he'd appear at the factory gates at dinnertimes, waiting for me to come out blinking in the strong light, laughing delightedly at the surprise on my face. I'd go off with him, Edgell Rickword's *Rimbaud* in my raincoat pocket. After he got married and his wife was expecting a baby I'd travel out to the Birmingham suburb where they were living temporarily with his in-laws, see the paintings he'd done to combat the sickening emptiness of his navy days and nights at Portsmouth—pictures of terror and innocence, soul dances, labyrinthine germinations, shooting stars, city nomad myths, done on cartridge paper unrolled on the floor of the Salvation Army hostel where he stayed at night to keep clear of the navy barracks. I read a prose poem he'd composed and called 'The Man Who Flew With the Birds'—and went dipping and gliding in pure flight on the curve of his vision. He was another autodidact, he went at everything blind. Instead of setting to work lucidly, in a civilised manner, he used his body, all his organs, holes, juices, nerves. He vibrated, made pictures, gave signs, in a pouring, helpless, signalling dance of prodigality. He was frantic, he was desperate, generous, felt doomed, no time—the fundamentals were in disorder and he was driven to these spasms of frenzied activity. Every move he made, every jitter echoed deeply in me. His wife had a young brother, and a little sister, seven or eight, who'd stare at me intently and say 'Aren't your lips red!' I'd reply 'Yes' and that would be the signal for a barrage of questions. 'Why are they? Do you use lipstick? Where d'you live? How long are you staying?' They were all crowded in this semi-detached, driving each other politely mad, and I'd say good-bye all round and leave, go trailing back to the main road with Ray, hearing him out to the bitter end, his despair so complete he could bang his head against the wall, his ballsed-up young civvy life, baby, wife, jeopardised by a chronic lack of money and free time and living room, his tribulations at the carpet cleaning factory, which was a dairy next time I went, a filling station the time after that—and I'd leave him at the corner wild-eyed, puckering his forehead, and I was sick at heart as I thought of him bowed down with worries and responsibilities at twenty, though not alone like me. I'd have changed places with him like a shot, that was the saddest and funniest part —not now, I wouldn't, but then, oh yes. Off I strode up the main road into nowhere, up the Brummagem Road walking blind, my back to the Black Country, my mind a seethe of impressions, thoughts, past the gigantic rampant tiger snarling full tilt out of the advert on the hoarding, on and on, the airport signpost looming out of the shit and drizzle and I shook my head and woke up, staring at it blankly like a sheep. Paris, that way; Rome, that way; Vienna, that way; New York, London, Brussels . . .

A Midland Red was coming, lit up, trundling along comically, two rooms on wheels—one up, one down. It scoured through the wet murk and I heard it, turned and waved it down. Not a soul upstairs. I felt empty and trembly and sick right through. The conductor came up and I stammered out something. I sat still against the window, quiet and obliterated. Going anywhere. Home. I let the bus take me, like having an Anywhere Ticket, while I travelled inwards, backwards. It was somewhere to go, it didn't mean anything more than that. I was going home again.

And I kept travelling, seeing the married woman. *Autumn Leaves* on the coach radio—' the red and gold '. Saturday night was my night; once every two or three weeks. She opened a new door on life. Her local bus would be late and I'd arrive in good time and wait on the corner, crucified. She came in for three hours: I travelled 120 miles altogether for my three-hour ration, then often her bus was late; the boy had measles, the clock was wrong, the dog had disappeared, the dinner had gone up in smoke. Domestic complications, tragedy, disaster. Two hours fifty minutes left. She came—how could she look so happy?— and then we needed another bus for the river: what time was the next one? We stood under the tin sign, that someone had heaved a brick at and buckled, tense as magnets not quite touching. My first woman. Mine—wonder of wonders. What could she see in me? She kept smiling, knowing and mysterious, the Egyptian eyes with blue eye-shadow glowed, digging into me, swallowing me. She mastered me without effort by her attack, her boldness. Her proud haunch brushed against me as if by accident. Her head was scarved, haughty, the face masked in war paint. I let out a passionate groan : ' Come on, bus!' and I could see her exult.

' Why such a hurry?' she whispered, gleaming with triumph and pleasure. Opposite, high on a tower of scaffolding, a corner of tarpaulin had ripped free. The north wind tore into it and it exploded, sharp as a pistol shot. *Crack-crack!*

Three hours she was giving me. She had nothing to lose. She was spiced and freshened by intrigue. I would go into the formalin of a poem of hers later. I'd be entered in her secret diary as an affair. She played the captivating, dangerous part in a fantasy she was weaving even as she stood there : the process continued, under my nose or wherever she was. And I took on new qualities in my own eyes. My silences became attributes, an actor's gifts; they were inspired pauses, charged with beauty and sex and death. She adored my urgency, I sensed that. So I hissed and groaned out loud to convey my grief at time passing. Displaying the anguish I felt gave me a kind of desperate pleasure. The cruellest thing was, I knew she was superbly immune. It was up to me to grab every minute that was going. My time was running away, being breathed away, talked and laughed away. The thought of it drove me wild. I was starving, she had meals galore. She was bored to distraction because she had everything. The situation ran along her nerves and she bristled excitedly. It was like the black river flowing invisibly, where we always went, the footpaths hairy with bushes at the openings, the trees spaced dramatically. She loved anything that fed her romanticism. Behind her, through the door she opened, only a year away, was Aline, with her morbidly sensitive mouth, melancholy gaze, her soft heavy thighs, her blossomy breasts set high up and wide apart, her girdle wrapped in brown paper and carried as a parcel so that she could stride better and feel free. Swaddled in a fur coat, bleakly married, she strode vigorously, swinging her free arm like a man. Her stocking tops shush-shushed as she walked. It gave me a feeling of opulent well-being to hear that dry regular sound chafing away; it was intimate and reassuring, homely and cheerful, that steady grasshopper friction. Summery, on the grisly winter cobbles. It lulled like the sea.

Crack-crack! The woman laughed richly, down in her throat. 'Time's whipping at us,' she crooned. 'Hear it?'

I heard it with tight lips, black heart. She was smiling at the imperious, swift whirling away of my minutes; she found it piquant. I looked at her, tongue-tied, struggling not to hate. I struck at her smile in my heart, to kill it. Then a 7 swung round the corner and surged at us, bull-like. At one stroke my bones were clad in a new body, I was all radiance, pride and gravity like a young king about to be married.

I muttered roughly, from my rapturous state : ' Let's get going.'

X